BATTLE ROYALE: SECRETS OF THE ISLAND BOOK ONE

BATTLE STORM

AN UNOFFICIAL FORTNITE NOVEL

CARA J. STEVENS

Sky Pony Press
New York

This book is not authorized or sponsored by Epic Games, Inc. or any other person or entity owning or controlling rights in the Fortnite name, trademark, or copyrights.

Copyright © 2018 by Hollan Publishing, Inc.

Fortnite® is a registered trademark of Epic Games, Inc.

The Fortnite game is copyright © Epic Games, Inc.

All rights reserved. No part of this book may be reproduced in any manner without the express written consent of the publisher, except in the case of brief excerpts in critical reviews or articles. All inquiries should be addressed to Sky Pony Press, 307 West 36th Street, 11th Floor, New York, NY 10018.

Sky Pony Press books may be purchased in bulk at special discounts for sales promotion, corporate gifts, fund-raising, or educational purposes. Special editions can also be created to specifications. For details, contact the Special Sales Department, Sky Pony Press, 307 West 36th Street, 11th Floor, New York, NY 10018 or info@skyhorsepublishing.com.

Sky Pony® is a registered trademark of Skyhorse Publishing, Inc.®, a Delaware corporation.

Visit our website at www.skyponypress.com.

10 9 8 7 6 5 4 3 2 1

Library of Congress Cataloging-in-Publication Data is available on file.

Cover design by Brian Peterson
Cover artwork by Alan Brown

Paperback ISBN: 978-1-5107-4433-2
E-book ISBN: 978-1-5107-4436-3

Printed in Canada

TABLE OF CONTENTS

CHAPTER ONE: ZANE

The transport vehicle bumped and groaned its way across the tracks. I craned my neck to get a first look at the battle school, but all I could see in any direction was other recruits, and above them, the tips of the windows showing a large expanse of sky. We were packed in, twenty cadets per cart, five carts in all. "These used to be commuter trains, back in the day," one know-it-all to my left announced to no one in particular, trying to start a conversation. No one picked up on it. The rest of the new recruits and I rattled along in silence, each lost in our own thoughts.

We were complete strangers to each other, and we each had our own reasons for joining up. Some were looking for an escape, others were seeking adventure, and some actually had a passion for the cause—or at least a passion for war. A rumor circulating around the station before we were herded onto the transport was that there was even a rebel aboard. I wondered how long it would take before anyone realized it was me.

"Where you from?" Just my luck, the know-it-all to my left picked me for his conversation target.

"The Outback," I said without looking over at him. I was still trying to get used to the universal translator an officer had shoved into my ear before I boarded the train. It itched like mad, but as soon as the circuits connected, I began to understand the noise of 100 people speaking fifty different languages. I briefly wondered where he was from, realizing that I was now hearing everyone speak Australian English through the translator. Possibly America, judging by his jeans, T-shirt, and white sneakers.

"The Outback as in Australia?" He sounded so amazed, I almost laughed. I would bet 100 bucks he had never met anyone from outside his own country, not to mention someone from a Southern continent before. I kept my lips sealed and just nodded. I didn't want to laugh at him, and I also wanted to keep my steely, tough-guy don't-bother-me look as long as I could. "I heard the rebel is from Australia," he said quietly, as if sharing a secret. I hadn't counted on the rumor mill being quite that fast.

Inwardly, I groaned. I had been hoping to keep my personal life a secret. Outwardly, I turned to face him with a steely glare. "And?" I said as menacingly as I could.

"Oh," he gasped, realizing at once that I was the person he was trying to gossip about. "Right. Well, it was nice meeting you." He looked around, trying to find an escape from the conversation that had gone so wrong for him so quickly. Unfortunately for him, we were packed tight as sardines and there was nowhere to run.

Might as well make this fun, I thought. "I didn't get your name," I said pointedly.

"Kevin," he said quietly. "And you're . . . ?"

"Not here to make friends," I replied, turning my back on him and staring out the window at the power lines crisscrossing the sky in a constant stream. I felt bad icing the guy out, especially in front of the rest of the kids on the train, but I really wished no one knew my backstory. Everyone else was anonymous out here. Why couldn't I be just another face in the crowd? I was just there to stay under the radar and check this place out without my family name causing people to suspect me for once.

The silence in the car was broken by an excited shout. "We're here!" Everyone pushed their way to the window so quickly, I felt the train car shift and sway from the weight of the bodies pushing to one side. I tried to remain cool, but I was just as curious and even as excited as the rest of them.

I stepped on my seat to see over everyone's heads and to my surprise, saw a vast desert with a bunch of wildly decorated buses topped with hot air balloons and literally nothing else. Where were the barracks? Where was the training ground? Where was the mysterious island that had been on the news feed day and night for the past year?

The train chugged to a slow stop, then shifted back, sending all of us crashing into each other. The doors squeaked open—they were sorely in need of some oil—and we all tumbled out into the sun, blinking, stretching, and breathing in the hot desert air. So, this was HQ. Not only wasn't it much, it wasn't anything. Were we supposed to live on those buses? Or maybe the buses were going to take us the rest of the way.

"Get moving!" a uniformed officer barked. We all looked up to see he was pointing toward a low sand dune just a few feet away. Like lemmings, everyone automatically started walking toward the hill.

Gosh, I thought, *are people that eager for instructions they'll follow any orders without thinking?* Then again, I looked around and saw there really were no other options, so I sighed and fell into step with the rest of the recruits. My mother's parting words sprang to mind for the first, but probably not the last, time: "Not everything has to be a battle, Zane. Pick them wisely or your entire journey will be an uphill struggle."

It turned out the dune was actually a hidden entrance. The heavy camouflaged door opened to a small, brightly lit entryway large enough for two uniformed guards and a computer station, with a second armored door leading down a long flight of stairs. I winced thinking about the idea of spending the next few months underground—no sunlight. No fresh air. No stars. What had I gotten myself into?

"It's not so bad once you're down there," a voice at my shoulder said. I turned to see a wiry tall kid with a rainbow-colored mohawk.

"I'd hate to know where you're from if you consider living in an underground bunker a step up," I replied with a laugh.

"Actually, I'm a city boy from South Korea—but my brother just came back from a tour and he said they've made it look and feel like you're living in a normal army barracks down there. Day, night, weather, parkour courses, the works." He looked me up and down. I realized I was doing the same to him. He stuck out his hand. "I'm Jin."

"Zane." We exchanged a quick handshake before the crowd pressed us into the room and toward the stairs. "What's with all the pushing?" I complained, flicking my shoulder to push off a hand that had come too close in the crush forward. "I didn't even get a chance to say goodbye to fresh air and sunlight."

"You won't even notice it's gone," Jin reassured me, laughing. *How could he be so confident?* I had no idea, but I did find it oddly reassuring. I'm not sure why, but I felt like I could trust this guy, and might even have liked him had we met under different circumstances.

"Thanks for the reassuring words. I hope you're right," I replied.

"I go to a boarding school and we eat, sleep, and have class on one city block. The buildings are connected, and sometimes I forget to go outside for days at a time," Jin explained. "Plus, I hear the food here is better than anything you've ever tasted. They feature dishes from all over the world for lunch and dinner! Their breakfast is purely American, though, so I'm going to have to get used to eating pancakes, pastries, and meat in the mornings."

"What's a pancake?" I asked. The unfamiliar word came through my translator.

"I think you'd call it a griddle cake or flapjack," Jin said. "My brother says they are *jjang*! That means super delicious in Korean. Slang doesn't translate, I guess."

A sudden surge of people pushed forward, separating us from further conversation. "Off we go! It was nice knowing you, Jin!" I called out, laughing.

"We'll meet again," he replied.

The rest of the day was a blur as ninety-nine dusty, hot, and tired recruits and I were funneled down a line, filling out paperwork and getting poked and prodded by three different doctors to make sure we were healthy enough to survive the program.

"It doesn't make sense," one girl just ahead of me whined. "I don't need a physical. I was the model for the recruitment poster, for heaven's sake. The scout said they only take people in perfect health, and I'm pretty sure everyone would agree I'm as close to perfect as it gets." She twirled, showing off her cosplay outfit—a short, all-white school uniform and high knee socks. I could tell she was one of those girls who pretend they're all cute, but would probably stab you in the neck with a ninja blade just for fun. She turned to see me looking her way. "You see?" she said loudly to the girl next to her. "People can't help but stare." She flashed me a big, white-toothed smile and wiggled her fingers at me. I wasn't going to take the bait, and hoped she'd go bother someone else, but apparently she liked people who played it cool. "I'm Zoe, by the way," she said to me.

"And you're next," I replied, directing her toward the tough-looking woman who was waiting for her to step up.

"And *you're* rude," she said, obviously offended that I didn't introduce myself to her. She turned and stalked off.

When my turn came, I walked into a small booth where a short, stocky man held my arm and started to scan me with a handheld meter. "I've just had three complete physicals and an IQ test. What could you possibly be checking that hasn't been checked twice already?" I demanded, squirming free from his grip.

"Uniforms and avatars," he said curtly, grabbing my arm back. He read my look—or perhaps anticipated my question since he had already had the same conversation with fifty other cadets before me. "Your uniform is for here at HQ," he explained slowly, as if he assumed I was a no-brain noob. "Your avatar that we send down to the surface for battle has to be a perfect match or the motion won't translate properly and you'll wipe out."

Okay, that, I didn't know.

He continued, lifting both of my arms and comparing them as if to see if they were even. "Even a millimeter off, and we'll have to scrub the suit, so hold still," he said, moving on to my left hand and inspecting it thoroughly. "Is this a tattoo, a scar, or just dirt?"

"A scar," I said quietly. It was the one from the first invasion. The one that had turned my parents against the government and into rebel operatives. The one that had turned my hair shock white before I was even old enough to discover what my hair color was supposed to be. I was too young to remember anything but a bright explosion and the loss of my favorite stuffed bear, but the scar stayed as a reminder that war was everywhere, even in a time of peace. As if I needed a reminder. My parents had been reminding me every day since. Of course, my white spiky hair was a constant reminder as well. Another reason I wanted to come here and get as far from home as possible.

The tailor's tug at my right hand brought me back to the moment. "These suits cost a fortune. Not sure why they bother. The acid rain washes 'em away eventually and then I have to start over."

The rain. I had forgotten about the poison storms that loop through the island. Some took just a few hours to start at the edge of the island and close in on an eye, while others took up to two weeks. Ever since the meteor hit, the air had been toxic—too toxic for ordinary humans to survive—and the skies rained down an acid-filled fog that closed in on the island from the outside into a different eye each time. Unpredictable and deadly, the rains had wiped out the island's population before scientists discovered the storm patterns and learned how to predict their timing and locations. The once beautiful and busy landscape was now a wasteland, useful only as a battle training ground for the young recruits who showed the most promise. We were here to train, controlling our avatars to see who would come out on top as the best tacticians, leaders, builders, scouts, and sharpshooters in a Battle Royale. It was all fun and games until your avatar got dissolved in the acid rain, I guess.

A final beep of the tailor's scanner told me his work was done. He waved me out of the room with a well-rehearsed parting phrase: "Assignments for your quarters and squads are on the wall to your left. No switching. No complaining. Meal rations will be taken in your common room tonight. You'll get your instructions in the morning."

"Don't forget to tip your tailor!" I mumbled, recalling a tagline from my favorite announcer.

"Hey, I know that one!" a happy voice called out. "'Make sure you hit LIKE and SUBSCRIBE!'" I looked up to see Jin grinning at me. "Did you get your assignment yet?"

I shook my head, walked over to the roster posted on the wall, and found my name. "I-28," I read out loud.

"What luck!" Jin shouted. "Same squad!"

His happy grin matched my own as I realized it was my first smile since I had left home. Maybe long before that, come to think of it. While I wasn't at combat training to make friends, having one would make this whole experience a lot more interesting. For the first time in a long time, I didn't feel lonely.

CHAPTER TWO:
JIN

"**H**ey, the games are starting!" someone shouted. I grabbed Zane's arm and pulled him into the throng of cadets rushing toward the large viewing screen. "Come on, we can see our room later."

"What's going on?" Zane replied.

"It's the graduation games," I answered, pulling him along to the stadium so we could get a good view of the screen. "The class ahead of us has one last mini-battle before they're shipped off to their assignments or sent home. The winner gets a week paid holiday and a special commission as soon as they get back."

I had watched the live feed hundreds of times from my computer at home, but sitting here in the stadium made it feel like I was seeing the battle for the first time. The battle buses left the depot, sending 100 avatars down to the island. We saw the path of the bus on the virtual map, and then watched as, one by one, 100 parachutes and gliders opened and the players floated down to safety. "What's up guys?" A familiar voice came through the speakers surrounding the stadium. "It's Rusty Pipes here, coming to you live from HQ stadium on graduation day. The cadets have left the battle bus and are hitting the ground running!"

A cheer went up around the stadium. We had all been watching and listening to Rusty Pipes for years, dreaming of our first day here right from broadcast central. Okay, maybe not Zane. I'd bet my life he was the rebel everyone was talking about, and I wondered what he was doing here at army training if he was so set against the government. I had never met a rebel before, and he wasn't at all what I expected. He seemed like a good enough guy, and he even seemed excited to be here. A true rebel would want to stay away from army training. A true rebel might even want to sabotage this place and blow it up. I hoped he wasn't a true rebel.

I checked the view screen and saw the hit count go up before the view cams even started to show the action on the ground. One player was down already. *"Fifi just fell thirty-nine meters,"* the news ticker read. Followed by another ticker reading *"Ogre trapped Ellie,"* and then *"Gunnar knocked out Curtis with a sniper (229m)."*

"The numbers are dropping fast here at our mini Battle Royale," Rusty called out gleefully. "Today's storm is a fast and furious one, folks, with only an hour to close in from the edges to the eye."

As he spoke, the camera panned over to Tilted Towers, where we followed a ninja avatar as she searched through the bedrooms in record speed. "Kellie-Mae is the favorite here today. She has a record number of eliminations and total wins for this year and . . ." Kellie-Mae's ninja avatar stopped to chug a shield potion. As she drank, footsteps rang out over the loudspeakers, and I held my breath. "Will she consume her shield in time?" Rusty's hushed commentary echoed my thoughts. Just then, a tough-looking soldier burst into the room carrying an assault rifle. Kellie-Mae wheeled around and took him out with a submachine gun. "Nice job, Kellie-Mae!" Rusty announced. The crowd went wild. I scanned the room, wondering, not for the first time, where the hidden avatar command center was located. I was so close to it, I was tempted to run through the halls and open every door I could find to see the real Kellie-Mae and everyone else controlling their avatars. But I was glued to the action just like everyone else. I'd find out soon enough, once my own Jin-suit got fitted. I hoped they got the rainbow mohawk right.

As I watched, the eliminations kept piling up. This was the fastest I'd ever seen people drop off. This was it for these cadets. They had trained together and separately all year, in duos, squads, and 50-50 teams, and it all came down to this solo battle. "Many will enter, one will leave," I said out loud.

Next to me, Zane nodded. "It's pretty epic, huh? And soon, we'll be down there just like them. Noobs battling it out among the ruins of a wasteland that used to be just another ordinary town."

"I know they say it was the meteor, but . . . well . . ." I stammered, trying to get my question out and hoping I wasn't being too forward by asking: "Do you think the government did this on purpose? I mean, since you're a rebel and all. Do you have any theories?"

Zane looked at me thoughtfully. "Are you a rebel?"

I shook my head. "Nah. I just pretty much question everything. My brother came back from HQ last year and hasn't stopped talking about it since. He felt like there was more going on than the people in charge were letting on. Like why we're going through all this training, you know? What's it all for?"

Zane never got a chance to answer, because just then a huge roar went up in the stadium as Kellie-Mae was eliminated by a sniper dressed as a graffiti artist. He hit her from ninety meters away. "I don't believe it!" Rusty yelled above the noise of the crowd. "And just like that, Kellie-Mae goes down. Thank you for your service, Kellie-Mae. See you in reruns!"

"Let's see who took down our top pick," Rusty announced. The screen flashed an image of the graffiti artist. His name tag read *Inky* and he was from Ireland. His record stood at two eliminations ever and zero solo wins. He might as well have been a noob. The screen changed to show some awesome graffiti artwork. "Kellie-Mae was eliminated by an almost unknown tagger named Inky. Chances are the guy mistook his long-range sniper for a spray paint can! Ha haha. Just goes to show you, it's anyone's game here at Battle Royale!" Rusty then cut over to a view of the golf course, where two players were racing All Terrain Karts across the field. "Speaking of which, looks like some people are just out for a joy ride on their last day on the Island," Rusty called out. The two players crashed their ATKs into each other and went flying, sustaining minor damage, but laughing as they ran off to find something else to play with.

The laughter stopped quickly as the two players looked up and saw the storm closing in. "Uh oh, guys, looks like rain!" Rusty announced cheerfully. "Hope you brought your umbrellas!"

The storm closed in, eliminating the ATK riders and a handful more players as Zane and I—and about ninety-eight other new cadets—watched in amazement as the cameras panned through the top locations on the island, following fighters, builders, and scouts. I was excited to see there were some fun parkour opportunities in Pleasant Park, and thought I saw something suspicious appear and then disappear quickly in Retail Row. I was looking at the map in a new light now that I was about to go down there and become a player instead of a watcher.

As the game went on, Inky went down without a fight thanks to a trap set by Minka, and suddenly it was just down to a battle between two players: Califa and Antonio. Califa had a legendary AR, and was building up a pretty strong wooden barrier against Antonio when he pulled out a grenade and blasted her foundation to shreds. Califa fell, taking minor damage, and hid under a parked car, not stopping to dress her wounds, while she waited for an opportunity. She didn't need to wait long. Antonio walked past and Califa took him out completely. As the drone came to collect Antonio's avatar, Califa busted out a round of Orange Justice—my personal favorite celebration dance. As I watched, the entire crowd started dancing as well! What a celebration! What a party! What a great time to be here at HQ. I couldn't wait for my chance to get down there, not just to uncover any strange mysteries that may be hiding on the island—I knew that was why my family had agreed to send me—and not just to bust out some crazy parkour moves with my avatar, but also to experience the feeling of being part of something so big and epic—a Battle Royale for the ages!

CHAPTER THREE: ASHA

The cheers from the stadium were almost deafening. I listened as Rusty what's-his-name announced the graduation games, and I tried to imagine the action as he called it, glad for something to keep me busy while I waited in the empty waiting room for alternates. I was the only one left. When the officer finally walked in, I jumped out of my seat with surprise, even though I had been staring at the door trying to will it to open for what felt like hours. "Asha!" she demanded.

I saluted, hoping that was the right response. "Yes, ma'am. That's me!" She eyed me cautiously. I held my breath, wondering if I was being called up or sent home.

"Cadet number forty-four failed out of placement. You're in if you can pass the course."

"YES!" I pumped my fist, then caught myself and slowly smoothed out my paint-stained shirt. "I mean, yes, ma'am. I'll do my best." She looked me up and down, taking in my tiny frame and probably making mental calculations of my odds at making it through. I knew she was trying to douse my hopes with her look, but it actually did the opposite. I was used to people judging me by my size and appearance, and nothing thrilled me more than to prove all the haters and doubters wrong. I looked her in the eye and asked: "When do I start?"

She led me through a long corridor to a practice arena so large, I couldn't believe it was underground. It was the length and width of a football field, filled with obstacles. The air was filled with a loud, steady hum, as if the air conditioners or machinery to run the whole base were just on the other side of the wall. I wondered what the course challenge would be, but whatever it was, I was ready. I had been training for months to get into Battle Royale—and to get the heck out of my small, backwards hometown in Kenya that was more of a watering hole than a parish. I had visited the big city, Nairobi, once in my life when I was five, and fell in love with the art and bustle of city life. I vowed I would someday become an artist and travel the world, leaving my mark everywhere I went. And to do that, I had to get down onto that island. So I practiced for months, only to become the lowest-ranked alternate in the qualifying round. Most kids had been recruited, but to keep things fair, the government offered a number of wild card spots where anyone who wanted to could try out. My parents thought I was crazy to go anyway, even though there was almost no chance I'd even get to run the course. My sister was even worse. "They choose the best from every corner of the earth, Asha. You are from a mud pit in middle-of-nowhere-Africa. They won't even see you, you're so small to them."

Perhaps she was discouraging me. Or perhaps she knew me better than anyone and knew her comments would only make me try harder to get in. Either way, here I stood. I put my climbing gloves on, cracked my neck and knuckles, kissed my left pinkie for good luck, and followed that dusty old officer out to the edge of the course. "What's my mission?" I asked, jogging in place to warm up my cold, unused muscles.

"Seventeen treasure chests, twenty-one minutes," she announced, holding up a stopwatch. "Ready?" I nodded. "Go!"

With the speed of a cheetah and the senses of a falcon, I began my race through the course, wondering why I had it so easy. No barriers? No problem! I made my way around the perimeter first, then circled in like a hawk. I saw chests gleaming in the inner circle, made a mental note of them, and kept to my course. When the shots first whizzed past my ears, they didn't register in my mind as gunshots. Then I saw the sniper on the roof up and to my right. *Ah*, so it wouldn't be too easy after all. Good. Now it was getting fun!

I did a barrel roll under a low overhang and counted the shots. Seventeen. He was rushing it and was almost out of ammo. I kept to the shadows this time, and fortune favored me as I came upon my first treasure chest. I tagged it with spray paint and moved on, soundlessly, through the buildings, staying under cover, and sticking to my plan.

I heard footsteps nearby and crouched behind a small bush. Without weapons or a shield, my only power was my size. My pint-sized stature looked to others like it would hold me back, but I wouldn't have it any other way. I was a master at hiding and fitting into small spaces. Both skills were perfect for this type of exercise.

I finished out my circle around the field, tagging fifteen, sixteen, and finally seventeen chests with minutes to spare. The lights immediately went up and the sergeant walked in, nodding her head but still not smiling. "Congratulations, Asha. You're our new cadet. Make your way to suite I-28 where you'll meet your squad-mates."

Sweaty and out of breath, I was grinning madly like a Cheshire cat. I wanted to hug the first person I saw . . . well, the first person after I left the unsmiling officer who gave me the news. I hoped my roommates and fellow squad members would be at least a little more approachable. And maybe more huggable, too.

CHAPTER FOUR: ZANE

Jin and I arrived at I-28 just as a worker was putting up a new name on the door and taking off an old one. "I guess Esme didn't place in," I said to the worker, but he didn't even look up. I squinted to see the new nameplate. "Asha," it read. We were a squad of five, which struck me as a little odd. I turned to Jin. "Aren't squads supposed to be in sets of two, four, twenty, or fifty?"

Jin nodded. "We end up in squads of four after the first week or so. Until then, we all work together, compete with each other, and try to either rise up or not fail out." He entered the room and I followed him through a sparsely decorated common room with a table and five chairs and an uncomfortable-looking couch. "They put us in teams of five at first in case someone sucks so badly, they get sent home, or is such a genius at this that they can get promoted. Squads that still have five after the first couple of weeks drop a member and form new squads of four with the leftovers."

"But that's never happened in the history of this place." We turned to see who spoke. A tough-looking buff girl with a scar on her cheek was coming out of one of the bedrooms off the common room. "And it's probably not going to happen for the first time here. I'm guessing we lose more this first week than any other cadet class, judging by how soft these noobs look." She looked us up and down with a critical eye. "You guys included."

Ugh. *Nice to meet you, too,* I thought, sarcastically. Out loud, I challenged her. "And you are?" I narrowed my eyes, trying to look and sound tougher than I felt. This girl looked like she would eat me and Jin alive for breakfast given the chance. Tough as nails was the first description that came to mind.

"Blaze. Third generation cadet. Pleasure to have you on the squad, Rebel. You, too, Acrobat."

"You know about us?" Jin asked cautiously.

"You two are open books. I made it a point to study the new cadets to see what I'm working with. Our other two companions are more of a mystery. It's a shame about Esme. She came from a good military family, too, like me. She was a wizard scout and a darned good scavenger," Blaze said appreciatively.

"Whatever she did well, I'll do better, guaranteed." A pint-sized girl covered in spray paint walked in grinning widely. "I'm Asha."

"You're the alternate?" Blaze asked. "You're bunking with me. You get the top bunk. I like to sleep with my feet close to the ground."

Asha shrugged. "Sounds good to me, roomie. I like it up high. Makes me feel tall!"

"I'm Zane." I offered my hand and Asha took it, shaking it warmly. "From Australia."

"I can tell," she giggled. "And you are . . ."

"Jin." Jin extended his hand for a shake, and Asha went in for a hug, surprising him and catching him off-balance.

"Sorry," she shrugged. "I'm a hugger. You'll get used to it!"

"I'm going to put my stuff down. Nice to have met you both," I announced and walked into the second bedroom. There were three beds. The top and bottom bunks were empty. The third, a single bed, was occupied by a tall, lanky teen, staring at us wordlessly when we walked in. He was wearing a long trench coat, and had long, dark hair that fell over his sleepy-looking, heavy-lidded eyes. "Oh, hi," I said, startled to find our third roommate was already settled into the room. He nodded his head in my direction and then glanced over at Jin, looking him up and down.

"Uh, hi," Jin echoed. I wondered if I had sounded as awkward. I wasn't sure what this new guy's talent was, but it must have had to do with putting people ill at ease. "I'm Jin. This is Zane. Are you Jaxon?"

"No one calls me that. It's Jax," he growled. "And make sure you keep off my bed and out of my stuff. Just because we share a room, doesn't mean we're gonna be best friends, staying up all night laughing and gabbing about our fears and dreams."

"Well, this should be a fun party, huh Zane?" Jin joked, which made me even happier that I had him for a roommate.

"ATTENTION!" Blaze's voice came booming from the common room. Jin and I rushed out. Jax didn't seem to move—he just kind of appeared effortlessly in the doorway. "Officer Gremble on deck!" Blaze called out.

We arrived to find a short, stocky uniformed older man greeting Blaze with a firm handshake and a pat on her arm. "How are you doing Blaze? Your father asked me to come check in on you and be sure you have everything you need."

"Yes, sir. Thank you, sir. It's all A-OK here. Everyone's present and accounted for."

"Excellent," Gremble said, his eyes roaming across all of us, sizing us up. His gaze rested on Jax. "I'm glad to see you made it here, Jaxon. A wise choice to take this assignment over juvenile hall. Mind you keep your behavior in line, or you'll find yourself in a deeper mess than when you arrived here."

Jaxon just stared at him. The officer walked over to stand toe-to-toe with him. "When I speak to you, you will respond. Is that understood?"

"Yes," Jax said sullenly. With a withering glance from Gremble, Jax corrected himself. "Yes, sir."

The officer walked to the door and looked back at them. "This isn't a social call, by the way. Your suits are ready. You can report to the battle room as soon as you get the call. It's time for your first trip to the island." He looked around at the five of us as we stared back at him in disbelief. I thought it would be days or even weeks before we got sent down there. It appeared we were about to be thrown into the fire— or the eye of the storm, to be more precise.

"So soon?" Asha asked, echoing my thoughts, her voice tinged with excitement.

"Yep. Turn left and take the blue hallway to the avatar room," he directed us. "This one's a mini-battle," he explained. "It's a short storm that lasts only an hour. Just enough time to show what you can do . . . and what you can't." As he walked out, he called over his shoulder: "Good luck, cadets! You're going to need it!"

Jin shook his head in wonder. "I'm sure Gremble knows it's ridiculous to just send us straight into battle so soon after arriving. Even if it is a mini-battle. Don't you think?"

In fact, I had thought about it and about everything surrounding these battles a lot. The thing was, I was no closer to figuring it out than I had been back home. There had to be a reason, and I knew I would eventually find it if I was patient enough.

CHAPTER FIVE: BLAZE

"**T**en-minute warning!" the loudspeakers blared. Jin, Asha, and Zane looked around in surprise, as if they were waiting for further instructions. Like baby chicks, they were looking for a mother hen to follow. Jax, on the other hand, just kept staring moodily as if he hadn't heard. He thought he was a lone wolf, but I could tell when it came down to a battle, he would end up looking to me for leadership as well.

"That means it's time to go," I barked at them. "Let's go, people!" I was the one with the army experience in the group. It was up to me to marshal these unfit cadets and get us to our battle stations on time. I stormed out of the barracks, leaving the door open for them to follow.

Asha ran ahead. She was small and speedy, which would make her a great scout and scavenger, but she had no impulse control, which meant she would need training and discipline. As much as I wanted to follow her lead and get there as quickly as I could, I walked slowly and with purpose, just like a soldier should. This was it—the moment I had been training for and dreaming of since the avatar program was first announced. I had heard that the simulator felt so real, you could actually feel the impact of jumps and hits, and even take minor damage while you were at the controls. I couldn't wait to try it myself. I knew I'd be a natural at it. After all, I'd been training for this my whole life. I wanted so badly to run through the houses at Snobby Shores and check out the crater at Dusty Divot, Tomato Town, Tilted Towers . . . I wanted to see it all. And I was about to go in!

Five other squads rushed past me and one hulking mass of a soldier pushed me so hard, I slammed into the wall. "Out of my way!" A hand reached up from behind me, pulling him back by his collar. "Ladies first!" Jax growled at him.

"She's no lady, she's a soldier like the rest of us." The neanderthal stalled and looked me up and down. "If you're expecting special treatment, sweetheart, you're headed for the wrong Battle Bus." He pushed past everyone else and disappeared into the room.

I caught Jax's arm as we entered the room. "I don't need defending."

Jax and I were stuck face-to-face in the crush of the crowd trying to funnel into the narrow doorway. "I defended our *squad*. I didn't defend you. He'll think twice before messing with . . ." his words trailed off as we entered the avatar room. Even Jax, mister "play-it-cool," was impressed. The room was enormous—like a giant cavern. It was laid out in a large circle, with twenty doors around the perimeter. Each door was set into a glass-paneled office with five control centers—one for each squad member. This was the avatar control center and there were no avatars or screens in sight. Weird. I scanned the signs and quickly found ours. "I-28, over here!" I called out to my squad. They followed like baby chicks to a mother hen, just as I predicted.

Our names were listed above each of the terminals. I quickly took my place at the center, glad that someone in charge recognized my leadership skills and experience. The rest of the team piled in and approached their spots. "Everyone, take your places!" A voice boomed over the speakers above our heads. The glass doors closed us in and we all stood in front of our consoles, wondering what to do next. It wasn't as simple as sitting down in a chair and taking the controls of a video game, which is what I thought it would be like. I can only explain it as a me-shaped station—the reverse of a kneeling chair. It looked like we were supposed to lean into it, and it would automatically support our bodies.

I placed my knees on the ledge and stuck my arms into the arm-holes in front of me. The console seemed to adjust to my presence, and it felt like a gentle cushion that also allowed me to move my arms and legs. I tilted my face into the blacked-out goggles, and a headset extended to my ears as a microphone slid into place in front of my mouth. I couldn't see, but I could hear my squad-mates perfectly through the headset.

"This feels so comfortable!" I heard Asha's voice.

"How does this thing . . . oh wait, I got it," Zane's voice came through next. "Can anyone see anything? Because I can't . . ." Zane's voice stopped short as a rush of cold air hit my face and my goggles cleared as if a fog was being lifted. "Well, I'll be stuffed!" Zane exclaimed. I guessed he saw it, too. It took a moment to register what I was looking at. I was on the party bus—or at least my avatar was. I had seen it a million times on the broadcast, so it was easy to recognize. My squad-mates were on either side of me, looking almost exactly like they did in real life. The computer readout in front of my eyes looked like the one on the first-person broadcasts. The readout reported there are 100 players and showed my inventory as empty save for a pickaxe and a glider.

"How do you move in this thing?" Jax asked. His avatar was staring straight ahead but his lips were moving.

"Try turning your head," Jin suggested.

Jax's avatar head turned smoothly to face Jin. "Whoa. That is just totally messed up." He moved his hand up to his face and marveled at it for a second.

I tried to do the same, and found that controlling my avatar was as easy as moving in real life.

The bus jerked forward. I felt that, too, along with the rumble of the engine and the tires making contact with the ground. The bus gained speed and took off suddenly as if it was going off a cliff. A cheer went up around the bus, and for the first time I noticed the other squads clustered near us. They were all getting used to their suits, staring at their hands and joking together as they made faces or tried to high-five.

I looked out the window and saw nothing but clouds. Then a monitor flickered to life, showing a map of the island and the trajectory of the bus. "We're in the Battle Royale!" Jin shouted. "Awesome!"

"We're just being thrown into this?!" Zane called out. "I haven't studied the map. I haven't been briefed. This is not good!"

"Stop your whining!" I shouted. "Just follow me. We'll all get off at the same spot and explore together. Most people will hop off at Tilted. You can find lots of loot, and it's close to the island's center, but it'll get crowded. I'd suggest starting at the farthest spot from the bus route—Looks like it's Lucky Landing."

"Sounds lucky to me!" Jin agreed.

The doors opened and I felt a rush of air just as if I were actually sitting on the bus. A cheerful girl standing by the open door in a basketball uniform turned to us, saluted, and waved. Then she tilted her head and was instantly swept out into the current. We all ran to the window to watch as her avatar raced headfirst down toward the island. Her glider popped out just before she hit the ground down at Paradise Palms. The rest of her squad jumped out to join her.

Jin stood up. "Let's go! We're at the prime launching spot for LL!" I would have liked to have been the one to announce it, but he was right. It was time to head down. As we stood by the doorway, I shouted above the roaring wind. "Asha, you take scout position. I'll be tactical. Zane, you're on collections. Jax, I assume you're our sniper and weapons guy?" He just stared back at me. "And Jin, you're our scavenger." Assignments handed out, I saluted them and headed out the door.

The sensation of falling at 300 kilometers per second is a rush I can't compare to anything. The wind roaring in my ears. The ground rapidly approaching like a blur. The feeling of panic. It's awesome and horrifying at the same time. I looked over and saw the rest of the squad was plunging to the ground at the same rate. "Turn hard to the left!" I called out as my glider popped up from my backpack. I grabbed the handles and steered it toward Lucky Landing.

"You're going too far!" Jin called out. "Pull to the right!"

I didn't realize he was talking to me until it was too late. I crashed, not in Lucky Landing, as I had planned, but near a giant toilet tower. "Flush Factory!" I groaned. What a noob mistake.

"Is this toilet towers?" Jin asked.

"I think you're thinking of Tilted Towers. This is a loo factory," Zane answered, laughing into his headset.

"Well, wherever we are, let's get a move on and see what we have to work with," I shouted, recovering from my first blunder. Zane immediately started hacking everything he could find with a pickaxe and we followed behind him, picking up the scraps of wood and metal we'd need to build.

"Found a chest!" Jin shouted from far off to the left. We rushed over and he parceled out bandages and weapons. Asha headed inside, while Jax headed up to the roof to stand guard.

I circled the main building, checking out the space for this and future missions. When I turned the first corner, I saw something gleaming in the distance. I ran up to it and discovered it was a chest. "Here's another chest!" I called out. It had a giant chug jug, which I drank quickly, looking around to make sure no one was nearby to hit me while I was exposed to attack. I also picked up a good defense weapon and some bandages. Not great, but useful.

Through my headset, I could hear gunfire. "Everyone okay?" I called out.

Jax's voice rang through slightly hoarse. "There's a sniper nearby. I'm headed down below. My weapon won't reach her."

"Grab a chug jug if you can," Jin called out. "My brother told me that taking a few seconds to drink a shield could save your life."

The count on my readout was already down to ninety. Ten people were already lost, probably because they steered their gliders into the ocean. It was too early in the game to lose in combat. But the numbers were about to start going down quickly. We hadn't had a chance to talk strategy or even assess how much experience everyone had before going in. I knew that every other team was facing the same challenge but still, this wasn't how I envisioned my first mission. Maybe we had a few moments for a meeting . . . "Meet me at the southeast corner. We should probably strategize."

Shots rang out through Zane's headset. "Kind of busy right now, Blaze," he shouted. "Blast!"

"You okay?" Jin asked. "I'm headed your way, Big Z."

I saw he was inside the factory, so I ran in. If he was hit, maybe we could take a few moments and chat while he bandaged himself up. I found them by a production line. Zane was crouched down, bandaging his arm. "Where'd you get hit?" I asked.

"Massive head wound, but somehow these bandages only go around my arms. Feeling a bit better, though," Zane said, reeling a little as he stood up. Jin reached out a hand to steady him. "Thanks, mate!" Zane replied.

A warning flashed on the screen. "Storm eye shrinks in three minutes fifteen seconds."

"We'd better head inland," Jin said. "I don't want to get caught in the storm."

I stopped him from running off. "We need a strategy. Let's just take a minute."

Jin shrugged free. "We don't have a minute. We'll talk as we go."

Asha ran up to us in a panic. "There you guys are! The storm is closing in. What does that mean? Where do we go?"

"Ramp," Zane said. "Follow me."

I didn't have time to argue—or ask what he meant. The other two trotted off after him and all I could do was follow. As I ran to catch up, I thought of all the things I would say when we were able to stop and regroup, starting with calling Zane out for taking off and not following the chain of command. When I arrived on the roof, Zane had already built an impossibly large ramp leading up.

"You're gonna get sniped," Jax said flatly. I hadn't even heard him arrive behind us. As if on cue, shots rang out next to us. I shot back, missing the target, but it stopped the rapid-fire attack. Zane ran up the ramp and the others followed. I considered staying behind in protest, but realized sticking together was the best bet.

While everyone else ran in a straight line, Jin flipped and bounced like a jackrabbit, whooping and hollering as he went. "Parkour! Boo yah! This is awesome!"

"Stay still!" I cautioned him.

But then Jax joined in—not with the bouncing and flipping, of course. He was too cool for that. But he zig-zagged his way up the ramp. "If you serpentine up the ramp like a snake, you are a harder target to reach. Surprised you didn't know," he said as he passed me.

He was right, of course. Studying this stuff and acing tests was one thing, I realized, but actually doing it—and in a fake body, no less, was definitely another. As I reached the top, Zane jumped off the ramp, popping out his glider and floating down toward Fatal Fields. Not my first choice of locations, I'd say, but we all followed suit, sticking together.

We landed in a wide-open field. Asha quickly threw up a few walls and a roof for protection. Impressive quick thinking. A suspicious-looking bush to my right started moving in my direction. I took it out with a shot as a message flashed on my screen: "Blaze knocked down Aziz with a rifle."

"You were almost am-*bushed*!" Jin called out, laughing.

"Nice hit," Jax said flatly, then ran off.

"Where are you going?" I demanded, annoyed that we still hadn't had a chance to discuss our plan. I would have liked to take a minute to build a fort so we could meet and regroup, but no one was following my lead.

"No time," Jax shouted over his shoulder. "It's a battle. I'm going in."

Jin, Zane, and Asha looked at each other and seemed to communicate without saying a word. They armed themselves, then took off after him. Once again, I found myself following instead of leading, silently seething and counting up our wrong moves in my head.

We never saw the grenade coming. My body was shaken by a searing pain that went from my toes all the way up to my eyeballs. A flash of light. Five drones hovered overhead. I found myself and my four teammates standing on a landing pad as messages scrolled across our view screens.

"Zoe eliminated Blaze with a grenade."

"Zoe eliminated Jax with a grenade."

"Zoe eliminated Zane with a grenade."

"Zoe eliminated Jin with a grenade."

"Zoe eliminated Asha with a grenade."

I suddenly became aware of my real-life body, as

the tension in my console eased and gently pushed me up to standing. I saw the rest of the team back in the room with me, stretching and rubbing their muscles back to life. My whole body ached and I was more tired than I had ever felt in my life.

"Well, that was SWEET, wasn't it? We did a fair bit of damage before we carked it!" Zane jabbered on in his Outback slang. "Good on ya for racking in a hit, Blaze!" He slapped me hard on the back, making me wince. I hadn't realized my back was sore, too.

I couldn't hold back my rage. "That was an embarrassing showing! We were terrible! That was pathetic!"

Jax put his hand on my arm. "Not here," he said gently. "Save it for the barracks." He was right, of course. The walls were made of glass and they were most definitely not soundproof. I looked around the avatar room and saw everyone still jacked into their terminals. We were the first team to lose. And probably the only team ever to lose at the same time from one shot. I knew my father would hear about this and I would never hear the end of it around the family dinner table. I wondered if it was too late to ask to be reassigned to another squad. I'd just have to set myself apart from these losers so well that they'd transfer me when it came time for the reassignments. Until then, maybe I could at least work on their skills to avoid further embarrassment in future battles.

We were forced to stand in the center of the room, watching the rest of the Battle Royale while one by one teams were eliminated and the storm eye shrank. Everyone looked as dazed as we felt, and the room was strangely quiet as we watched the last of the battle play out. A couple of avatars were lost to the storm, burning in the acid rain. It looked like it would take a while to refresh the suits, meaning those players would be out of commission for a while. No wonder they had extra cadets for the first few battles.

CHAPTER SIX:
JAX

When we got back to the barracks, all I wanted to do was crawl into my bed and sleep for ten hours. My muscles ached. My head was pounding. The others were complaining, too, or at least holding their heads and favoring the areas where they got hit. "I know it was my avatar, not my body that got hit. Why do I feel so awful?" Jin moaned.

I waited for Blaze, that know-it-all, to start reciting a long speech about brain-computer interface-virtual reality, but she just shrugged. "I don't know. I heard it takes a while to get used to it," she replied. "I'm going to get something for this headache. You guys should probably do the same. You all look terrible." She walked into the room she shared with Asha and then poked her head back out to give us a reminder. "Don't forget. Dinner is served at eighteen-hundred hours." That girl was always in military mode. I wish she would lighten up.

Zane grinned. Jin gave him a sideways look. "What makes you so happy? Don't you hurt all over, too, or do Australian rebels train themselves not to feel pain?"

"Oh, I'm right knackered right now, but the fact that Blaze has less of a Scooby Doo than we do, has me on the floor!" Zane was holding his sides laughing while Asha, Jin, and I just stared.

"Mind saying that in English for the rest of us? My universal translator doesn't speak Aussie slang," I told him.

"Sorry, mates. I meant to say I'm sick as a dog, too, but the fact that Blaze knows as little as we do cracks me up." Jin and Asha nodded in agreement, and I wasn't about to enlighten them. I went to my bed, lay down, put a cold, wet washcloth over my eyes, and tuned everyone out.

It's funny I was the only one who knew what these systems were and why they gave everyone such a headache. I hadn't known either, until the day before. I couldn't believe it had only been twenty-four hours since I had been caught jacking my neighbor's car because she had lost her keys down the sewer grate and was late to pick up her kid from daycare. The policeman caught me in the act and threw me into the back of the squad car before she or I could even explain—not that I was going to. I hated explaining myself to people, which is probably why I got into trouble so often.

Downtown at the station, the officer pointed to a bench and said: "Move from this spot and I'll lock you up for good," so I stayed. Hours passed. While I was worried at first about what was going to happen to me, eventually I realized there wasn't much they could do that would make matters worse than sending me back home. Eventually, I figured if they were talking about me, I should probably pay attention. They were debating whether to send me home and pretend they hadn't seen anything, send me to a juvenile detention center since it had been my third arrest in two weeks, or ship me off here.

The sergeant and the officers all agreed they'd all be happier and better off not seeing my face again for a year. And it would mean a lot less paperwork for them. They just had to run it by the social worker, and the social worker had a whole lot to say about it. "There's no evidence that a closed-loop EEG-based BCI-VR system won't have lasting effects on a teen's brain development." I had no idea what that meant, but it sounded bad.

"I have no idea what you're saying, ma'am," the sergeant admitted.

She went on to explain that BCI-VR is the brain-computer interface-virtual reality they used to control the avatars. The control center jacks into your brain waves, so when you think you're moving your own body, you actually move your avatar. And when your avatar gets hit, you feel the pain as if you were hit, too. Turns out that all that time parents spent protesting video games, they didn't know the army was doing even worse damage with a real-life game that hijacked kids' brains.

It would have been easy to side with her, but there was one reason I had to get on that transport. Cash. Turns out if I made it through the full year, I'd get a big check from all the screen time I'd get. Could even be enough to get my little brothers and sisters out of that apartment and take them away to a place with fresh air and sunlight. That's how I ended up here. But I wasn't about to tell all this to my uninformed squad-mates. Or tell them that the program they had waited their whole life to join, like it was some reality TV show, was actually one day going to fry their brains and hurt their bodies, too. I figured I'd play that card later if I needed it. In the meantime, being here, even with these fresh-faced, bickering kids, was a whole lot better than being cramped in a filthy apartment with too many relatives and not enough beds.

The bedroom door opened with a bang. "It's eighteen-hundred hours, what are you doing lying around? Let's move, people. Dinner's here and we have a lot to talk about." Blaze exited the room, leaving the door open for us to follow. I stayed in bed with my eyes closed. Maybe if I pretended to sleep, they'd leave me there or just forget about me.

"You know she'll just come back if we don't get out there, right?" Jin asked Zane. I hadn't known them for long, but they were already forgetting I was there, which was fine with me. No one expected anything of me, so no one would be disappointed. It gave me a chance to watch them all, unobserved. Jin seemed like a happy-go-lucky kid who just wanted to bounce off the walls, and Asha was a scrappy, fast little smiling thing, but I didn't know much about her, either. Zane was the most interesting one. He had an edge—when I could figure out what the heck he was saying. I heard some kids saying that his parents were some top spies who operated outside the law. Sometimes for the government and sometimes against. I could respect a guy like that—where you don't blindly follow what someone says just because they're in charge. But why was he joined up here, training to be in the army? Wasn't an army soldier the opposite of a rebel?

I felt a gentle shove at my boot. I opened one eye and saw Zane standing over me. "Come grab some food with us. You do eat, don't you?"

In response, I swung my legs down to the floor, stood up, and followed him into the dining area of our common room. The food actually looked good, and it smelled great. I realized I hadn't eaten since breakfast because my processing meetings ran long. I grabbed a fork and dug in, grateful that everyone was using their mouths to eat rather than jabber on.

"We should do a 'get to know you' session," Blaze announced after clearing her plate.

I glared at her. "If there were a window in this room, I'd try to throw you out of it right now."

"Your threats don't scare me," Blaze replied, jutting her chin out, but I could see she was a little afraid. A few words from me or Zane could break her illusion of control over our squad. Funny, after all she chattered on about her military training and background, she was still just a teenager who was trying on a personality like everyone else. "I was trying to make this pleasant, but if you're going to be like that, we can just cut to the real topic we have to discuss: what happened out there on the island."

"Fair dinkum. We really made a dog's breakfast out of this one." Zane shook his pork chop at Blaze, nodding in what I assumed was agreement.

"We were not all on the same page. We had no strategy. No one was listening to my instructions. That's why we lost," Blaze scolded us like she was the teacher and we were the students. I sat back in my chair and watched to see how the others would react.

"It was our first time down there, Blaze. It was everyone's first time. We can't be called out for being caught unprepared," Jin said defensively.

"No one elected you leader, Blaze. We had no reason to follow you," Asha added. I liked where this was going. I shut my mouth and watched the fireworks.

"If you really want to place blame, you should put your finger on your nose, Blaze," Zane said with his mouth full. "I mean, you dropped in the wrong spot and made us follow you. You kept trying to get us to stick together, which landed us all getting blown up together. And you had us stopping and standing still to strategize instead of just taking action and seeing what we could do." Zane put down his food and wiped his mouth. "And next time, we figure out our roles *together*. We're a team, not a dictatorship." With that, Zane stood up, took his tray to the compost chute, dumped it, and opened the door. "I'm going on walkabout. Anyone with me?"

Jin and Asha followed his lead, and the three of them took off, leaving me with Blaze, who looked like she might explode. "Don't take it too hard," I said. "It's the first day. Lighten up. It'll all shake out soon enough." I stood up, cleared my trash, and walked to the door. "I'm going to go explore a bit, too. Wanna come?" I don't know why I asked, but I was glad she shook her head no.

I walked off down the hall and I saw Asha and Zane laughing while Jin ran up the wall and used it to do a backflip. I smiled. Even though I missed my crazy mess of a family, especially my little brothers and sisters, I felt almost happy for the first time in a long time.

CHAPTER SEVEN: ZANE

Asha, Jin, and I walked through the hallways, but all we saw was a maze of locked doors. Jin was literally bouncing off the walls, showing off his parkour moves. Asha was eyeing the endless white-washed corridors and talking about how a blank canvas was an amazing opportunity for tagging. "I'd love to spray-paint this whole place. Everything is so dull. It's like they're trying to make it look as boring as possible."

"What do they expect us to do here when we're not training and battling?" I wondered out loud. "I haven't seen any of that cool technology you were telling me about earlier, where you can't even tell we're underground, Jin." I looked around. "It's actually pretty dark and depressing down here."

Jin scratched his head and shrugged sadly. "I think my brother may have misrepresented this place a bit, huh? Maybe it just makes the island look that much better to us."

"We haven't tried *every* door yet." Asha jiggled yet another door handle, just in case. That girl was so optimistic. She had tried at least thirty already. What made her think this one was going to be different? It wasn't, of course. "Ah shoot. They're probably locked because it's late and we're supposed to be in bed."

"Who can sleep? This is our first night! Our first time on the island! Wasn't it awesome? Can you wait to get back down there?" Jin was bouncing up and down again. Where did all his energy come from? My eyelids were drooping and I couldn't wait to get to bed.

As we turned the corner, a movement caught my eye. I turned and saw Jax loping along behind us at a safe distance. Why was he following us? "You guys notice we have company?"

Jin and Asha turned and saw Jax, too. Asha waved. Jax waved back uncertainly, then disappeared around a corner. "D'you think he was following us?" Asha asked.

Jin shrugged. "If he was, he isn't anymore. What do you think his deal is?"

"I think he wants to be left alone for now. He'll talk when he's ready. If he wants to," I said. Jax seemed like the street kids I hung out with back home. They didn't mean anyone any harm, and were happy to stay out of trouble by keeping to themselves. But, like a street kid, Jax seemed tough. It sounded like he had a criminal record from what the officer said. But there was something in the way Jax spoke that made me feel like he'd have our backs in a fight.

We walked a few more steps and were surprised to find ourselves back in front of our door. "Either this place is a circle, or we took a few wrong turns," Asha said, then shrugged. "Either way, I'm happy to be back here. I'm ready for bed!"

We went in and took turns washing up in the shared bathroom. I lay down in the bunk, happy to find it was actually pretty comfortable, and even happier to find that I was no longer sore and aching. I fell almost instantly into a deep, dreamless sleep.

I woke up to the sound of a trumpet blaring loudly through the speakers located in our main room. We all jumped out of bed and met in the common room, just as the announcement started. "Good morning, cadets!" the voice announced cheerfully. "This is Sergeant Velasco speaking to you from Avatar Central! I trust everyone had a wonderful night's sleep in their barracks, and you're ready to start the day. You'll find breakfast has been delivered to your door. We expect you all to be here in thirty minutes for introductions and our first playground session. See you soon!" The voice cut out. Asha opened our door and brought in the breakfast tray, piled high with eggs, bacon, sausage, flapjacks, juice, and freshly baked muffins.

"Yum! I think I'm gonna like it here!" I announced, grabbing a muffin and stuffing it into my mouth. It was warm and delicious and filled with berries. Jax did the same, while Jin, Asha, and Blaze sat down at the table, ready to have a civilized meal. "I don't think we have time for napkins and silverware, kids. We've gotta hit the road." I grabbed two sausage links and a flapjack in one hand and a glass of juice in the other. "Cheers!" I lifted my glass and downed it in one gulp, then stuffed myself with the rest of the food in my hands. "Dibs on the toilet!" I shouted and headed in to wash up.

"Disgusting!" I heard Blaze say as I closed the door. I could hear the three of them clinking silverware and chatting over breakfast. It almost sounded like a normal home. Or at least what I imagined a normal home would sound like. I mean, my family weren't barbarians eating with our hands, but my mum, dad, and I were more like strangers who shared the same house. They were off at odd hours and slept when they weren't working, fighting, or traveling. Food appeared in our larder, and the house was kept clean, although I rarely saw Neria, the housekeeper who kept our lives running in the background. I got the feeling she was the only one who really would notice I was gone, and I didn't even know her last name.

I finished washing up and opened the door to find Jax standing there, waiting, toothbrush in hand. "You're speedy. Good. I can live with that," he said and brushed past me into the bathroom. He was a bloke of few words.

I headed to the avatar room as soon as I was ready and watched the other cadets pile in. I recognized a few of them from the day before. Cheerful Kevin, the poor kid from the transport vehicle, and Zoe the model who took us all down with the same grenade. And the jerk who pushed Blaze. Look at me, getting to know the locals already. *Mum would be proud*, I thought to myself, smiling. The other members of my squad trickled in and met me by our control room door. At 8:30 sharp, an officer walked to the center podium, accompanied by Officer Gremble, the one who knew Blaze's father.

"Good morning again, cadets! It is nice to meet you all in person. I am Sergeant Velasco. Mine is the first voice you will hear each morning. It is the voice you must listen to at all times if you want to succeed and get ahead, and it's also the voice you must heed if you do not want to get booted from this program. So, listen carefully and you will do fine.

"We held our first surprise Battle Royale yesterday. Many of you really sucked up the farm. Some of you missed the landing from the start. Others tried to blow up their own teammates. Some of you got a chance to feel the sting of acid rain for yourselves. And one entire team actually got eliminated by the same grenade!" He paused as jeering laughter filled the room. My squad-mates and I exchanged horrified looks.

"Oh man, that was us!" Jin whispered to me. Blaze silenced him with a stare.

"But luckily, none of what you experienced counts much toward your record." I saw Blaze let out a relieved sigh. "We didn't expect you to battle like masters your first time. Today, you will hit the play-ground. You'll have one hour to explore the island with no penalties and no permanent eliminations before the storm hits. If you get knocked out, your avatar will be beamed back in, as long as your suit doesn't sustain extensive damage. The only excep-tion is if it gets caught in the rain for too long. That ruins a suit and you'll be docked at HQ until your suit can be repaired.

"There is one catch," he said and then paused for effect. "You will be getting on the bus in ranked order, from most impossible odds to best so everyone can see where they stand."

This was not going to be good, I thought. I tensed, waiting for the words I knew were about to leave his mouth.

"I-28!" he shouted. A spotlight shined on us down from the ceiling. All eyes were on us. "You were the first team eliminated. You have the honor of being first." My face reddened. Jin and Asha took it in stride, waving happily to the others in the room.

Blaze whispered out of the side of her mouth, as if she thought no one would see her even though all eyes were on us. "Stop that! You look like idiots!"

"We look like idiots anyway," Jin whispered back. "Better to own it than be embarrassed."

Jin was right. I lifted my hand, waved, and smiled along with him. Why not own it? It would play out better in the long run. Sergeant Velasco went through the rest of the teams, listing them from last to first, then our glass doors opened and we filed inside.

I entered the control console, wondering if it were going to be as tough on our bodies each time we went in, or if it would get easier over time. I wiggled my fingers and toes and steeled myself for the transition. I was about to find out.

We were alone on the battle bus, and everyone looked pretty bummed out. "Cheer up, mates!" I tried to sound chipper. "There's no place to go but up when we're faced with impossible odds, right?"

Jin nodded, then jumped out of his seat. "That's what we should name our squad—The Impossibles!"

"That's a stupid name!" Blaze shouted.

"I love it!" Asha and I said at the same time.

"Fine by me." Jax shrugged.

"You're ridiculous. We need something powerful. Something . . . something the opposite of what you said," Blaze sputtered, trying to regain control.

I leaned in closer to Blaze. "Pick your battles, mate," I said quietly. She opened her mouth as if to argue, then seemed to think better of it. "Just go with the flow," I added.

The bus filled up and then we were off, soaring into the sky. Soon, we were in position above Tilted Towers. "Let's get out here," Blaze said. "It's got good loot and it's the best battleground for noobs like us."

Without argument, we all stood up and followed her to the door. That seemed to cheer her a bit. We jumped out and dove, along with half of the other recruits on the bus.

We landed together on a black-topped roof in a courtyard that looked like it was part of a double L. I immediately picked up the first weapon I found. It was a sniper. *Rough luck*, I thought. I'd pick up something better later. Jin hacked at the roof and we dropped down into a room filled with weapons and supplies. Blaze chugged a large shield and tossed me and Jin each a small one. Asha scouted the next room and called out when she found a chest. Jax covered us with another powerful close-range weapon as we made our way through the building.

I heard footsteps, turned and hit the person next to me, realizing with great satisfaction whom I had just knocked down. *Payback's fun, isn't it, Zoe?* I gloated as I rushed past her avatar lying on the ground. Jax hit her again, getting her beamed back up to the drop zone, and I snagged her weapons and ammo. This had turned into a nice, old-fashioned feud with that girl. We made our way down the building, sometimes taking the stairs and other times hacking through the floor and jumping instead. The rooms were filled with loot, as Blaze had said. We moved quietly, pointing out finds or warning each other of dangers. We had to take this seriously from now on.

We exited to a park. I heard bullets whiz past me, turned and blindly fired a round in the direction they came from. I realized with some satisfaction I had hit three cadets in one burst. All from the same team. While there would be no eliminations this round, a hit still felt pretty good. I saw the drones beam them up and watched as they glided back down from the sky.

There was a sound coming from under the red bricks beneath my feet. I saw Jin looking down as well. We both hacked at them, and were pleased to find a hidden chest beside some old pipes. It was filled with loot. We grabbed it and divided it among the rest of our squad, then moved down a south path that led to a stairway. "This is the way to Shifty Shafts," Asha said as we ran down the stairs. I was glad someone was paying attention to the map on the view screen. I was focused on keeping an eye out for movement in the distance. I didn't want to get ambushed again, especially if Zoe and her team were out there some-where looking for payback.

I saw something moving down below and shot at it, only to hear Blaze's angry voice buzz in my head-set: "Zane, you idiot, stop shooting at me and get the guy on my tail!"

I adjusted my aim and tried again, scoring another hit. "Sorry about that, mate. Didn't know you were down there."

"It's okay. I'm collecting his loot now. He was loaded!" Blaze called back.

We met up down at Shifty Shafts and entered the tunnel together. There wasn't much loot, but we ran into another squad just standing around. They must have been talking through their headsets. They all turned to look at us when we entered. One put her hands up to show she meant no harm. I nodded, and so did Jin and Asha. Jax lifted his gun, but Blaze had him lower it. "It's just a meeting, Jax." We left the maze of tracks and went up to ground level.

The layout above was just as complicated, with broken-down shacks, more tracks, and stairs leading nowhere. It seemed like a great place for a game of hide and seek, and a terrible place to go if you didn't have the right weapons to defend yourself. Jin threw down a spike trap as we exited the cabin. "Think of it as an un-welcome mat for the next visitors," he joked.

Blaze shook her head at him. "We're not here to rack up eliminations, Jin."

"We're here to sharpen our skills, Blaze. Spikes are sharp, aren't they?" Jin trotted off to the east.

My stomach growled, meaning we had been down here for a while and it was getting close to lunchtime. "How much time do we have left?" I asked.

Blaze looked up at the sun. "Twenty minutes."

Jin looked up at the sun as well and challenged Blaze. "How can you tell what time it is by the position of the sun?"

Blaze shook her head. "I can't. I was just clearing my visor. There's a countdown on your goggles."

Asha laughed. It seemed that girl was always looking for a reason to smile. "We all have a lot to learn, don't we?"

We followed Jin to the east and saw a small town. "What's that spot?" I asked Asha. She seemed to have a grasp of where we were at all times.

"I know that's Salty Springs, but for some reason my map just disappeared from my visor," she replied, tapping on her forehead. "Ouch. I forgot my avatar isn't actually wearing a visor."

"You just dropped off my map, too," Jin noticed. "I mean, I'm looking at you, and I can see you, but your name doesn't appear like the rest of the squad does."

"First glitch of the game," Asha said cheerfully. "I'll be fine. I know my way around pretty well. We'll just stay in touch."

I looked around at the town of Salty Springs. It had a few houses and a watchtower, as well as a petrol station labeled PASS 'N' GASS. I pointed it out to Jin: "Look. A fart joke!"

Jin laughed and shot at the sign. Blaze gave him another stink eye. "What?" he asked innocently. "It's target practice. It can't hurt."

We quickly found out he was wrong as a grenade was powering toward us. Jin's shot had given our position away to the enemy. Jax built a ramp and we dove under it just in time, sustaining only minor damage. Blaze was impressed. "Quick thinking, Jax."

He simply nodded, then built another ramp, running up it with his weapons drawn. "Let's go take out whoever did that." I jumped into action and the others did as well, and we had a proper gun battle with an opposing squad. We alternated between shooting, reloading, and building, and I noticed our opponents' tower was getting higher as well. I was out of wood. In my excitement to explore the island, I had forgotten to keep collecting. Fortunately, I still had plenty of weaponry and was able to keep up our offense as my squad-mates built and defended our turf.

Our stalemate ended only when the storm began to move in. The opposing squad jumped down from their fortress and ran toward the eye and we did the same. Just then, my headset crackled and buzzed, and another voice came through as if from far away. "Setting coordinates . . . they're on the move. Headed toward the crater . . ."

Another voice cut in: "Wrong channel! Move over!"

The first voice came back: "Gah!"

Then a burst of static crackled through the headset, followed by Jin's voice, shouting: "What in the world was that? Who's on our com?"

"It's HQ. They're obviously monitoring us," Blaze replied snidely.

"That clearly wasn't HQ. They were tracking us. I'm sure of it." Jin was freaking out, walking in circles and putting his hands to his head. "They're watching us."

"Who do you think is watching?" I asked cautiously. I wanted to believe Blaze, but I also believed deep down that there was more to this place than the officers were letting on and the advertisements were telling us. Was this really evidence of something bigger, or just a low-level communication mistake? I wasn't certain.

"What do you think, Asha?" Jin asked, looking around for her. "Hey, has anyone seen Asha?"

I shook my head. I hoped we hadn't left her back in the storm area. "Her com still isn't working. She's not on my map," Blaze replied. "But she's a big girl. She'll find her way back to us."

I looked back at Salty Springs but all I saw was a shimmering wave of acid rain. I hoped she wasn't back there, and if she were, I hoped she could make it through.

"We need to go back for her," Jin cried out, panicked.

Blaze was about to protest, then agreed. "We do need to stick together."

"That's nonsense," Jax replied. "This isn't even a real battle. She can't get into any trouble. She'll get sent back up and we'll meet her there."

I agreed with Jax. We were two against two. "I'm going back," Jin insisted. "You guys can go on ahead and keep exploring."

I shook my head. "If you go, I go. We're a squad."

"But you don't agree with me?" he asked. I had the feeling that the only thing causing him to doubt himself right then was me. He trusted my instincts. Possibly even more than I did.

I shrugged. "Heck, it's just a game, as Jax said. Might as well go back for her and stick together."

We headed back into the storm. An acid mist began to enclose us. Wherever the mist hit my suit, there was a slight hiss as the avatar took damage from the rain. I looked over at Jin, who seemed determined to enter the rain to save Asha.

"She might even be zeroed out by now," Jax said. "Once she gets knocked down, her avatar health goes down. When it hits zero, she gets beamed back up automatically."

"I'm not stopping!" Jin headed farther into the edge of the storm.

The rain pelted my suit and my skin began to burn. My health bar was falling quickly. I looked over and the others were taking the same damage. Through the rain, I saw Asha. She was standing safely in the eye of the storm. She was covered in spray paint and she was shouting at us just as her com kicked back in. "What are you idiots doing in there? I can't get in to save you!"

We all looked over at Jin, who looked horrified. He curled up into a ball and let the rain hit him until his health bar depleted. I tried to make it back out to the edge of the storm, but it was too late. I zeroed out and my visor faded to black. I opened my eyes and was back in the control room, backing out of my suit and feeling the sting of acid rain as if it had hit me directly.

CHAPTER EIGHT: ASHA

I stood in the control room watching as one by one my squad-mates came out of their command centers. They looked awful. I was about to rip them to shreds for heading into that acid rain. But when I saw their faces, all I could feel was sympathy. "You're covered in red sores! You poor fools. Didn't your mamas ever teach you to come in out of the rain?"

Jin looked up at me sadly. "I thought we had lost you back in the rain. We went in after you."

I hugged him gently. "Silly boy. I just went off to tag a nice whitewashed wall with spray paint. My GPS and com were down and then the suit flashed a malfunction warning. A drone beamed it back up to HQ and I ended up back here. My suit is in for repairs now."

"You could have let us know," Blaze said accusingly. "You shouldn't have left us once you knew your com wasn't working."

I didn't have time to respond. The door flew open and Sergeant what's-his-face stormed in. "What did you people do to my suits?" he demanded. His friendly, happy tone was gone, replaced by seething anger. "This was supposed to be a harmless drill, but now your suits need to get detoxed from the acid rain. You're all docked until tomorrow!" He wheeled to look at me and pointed a stubby finger in my face. "Except you. You get to go down alone in a solo challenge along with the rest of the cadets." He didn't wait for a reply, but stormed out as angrily as he had entered.

"We are in very hot water." Jin shook his head sadly. "I'm amazed he didn't boot us from the program for this. We're two for two in terms of fails."

"That's why we're The Impossibles!" I laughed, reaching up to put my arm around his shoulder. "Don't worry about it. We lived to fight another day. I've got this." My stomach growled. "Anyone else hungry?"

Blaze checked the schedule that had been tacked to our wall while we were in the battle. "Looks like lunch is next. It's in the mess hall. After that, you get to do the solo battle, Asha. Without us," she groaned. This must have been so hard for her, poor girl. She had trained her whole life for this and I think we were a big disappointment to her.

Zane stretched his sore muscles and yawned. "I'm brown bread from that last battle. I could use a nice big sanger!"

Brown bread? Sanger? That boy had more strange expressions than I could count. Most of his words weren't getting translated through my universal translator implant! I assumed brown bread meant toast, like feeling burnt out. That's how I felt. Maybe a *sanger* was a sandwich? We walked out with the rest of the recruits and found the mess hall not too far away. It was a big cafeteria with trays and stations for hot and cold food from all over the world. It smelled wonderful. Not just because I was hungry. Looking around, I vowed to taste every country's food at least once before training ended. On the menu from the African continent, I was pleased to see a Kenyan Pilau—spiced rice—and corn and bean stew, but I kept walking. I wanted to eat food from the farthest place from my home. After circling each station, I finally grabbed a cheeseburger and made a mental note of the sushi for dinner.

The noise of 100 hungry cadets was overpowering, especially for a small-town girl like me. I took my burger to the farthest edge of the room and walked into an alcove filled with empty boxes.

Alone in relative quiet, I was able to take a moment to relax and unwind. I took a bite of my cheeseburger, but I didn't have long to enjoy it. The lights flickered and Sergeant Velasco's voice rang out over the loudspeaker. "Five-minute warning!"

No matter where I go, there's no hiding from his booming voice. Or the battlefield, I thought, wolfing down the rest of my burger. I wanted to avoid the rush back to the avatar room.

It was weird in the control room without my squad-mates. I waited for the announcement and jacked into my station. I vowed to do my best and make the team proud. On the battle bus, I felt the others look-ing at me as if they knew I was the sole player from my squad in this solo battle. The odds were against me, but that was always when I performed my best.

The map showed a new path that went directly over Tilted Towers. I decided to play it safe and hit that spot first, even though that was where most of the other cadets were going to land their avatars as well. I knew the place and had already built a map of it in my head. I was lucky that way—I could go somewhere once and then picture the map perfectly in my mind. I just hoped they had managed to repair my suit properly. I didn't have a mind map of places I hadn't been yet!

I aimed my glider at a black rooftop and instantly picked up a pretty decent weapon and some ammo. Other gliders were coming in quickly, so I smashed through the roof and walked through the rooms, checking to see if the chests, ammo, and med kits were in the same spots as before. Since I was solo, I realized I'd have to collect building materials, too, so I hacked at the furniture and collected some wood and metal as I made my way down.

Every time I heard footsteps, I hid behind a door and waited silently for someone to pass on by or come in. I picked up a spike trap in one of the rooms, and threw it up on the wall by the stairs so no one could follow me. By the time I hit the ground floor, I had knocked down three players and eliminated two. Unfortunately, the next part would be harder as a solo player—running through the field from the apartment complex to the next stop. But what should my next stop be? I hadn't studied the map. I began to panic. Suddenly a voice in my ear whispered: "I hear Dusty Divot is nice this time of year."

"Jin!" I shouted. "Where are you?"

"I'm up in HQ. Zane's here, too."

I was happy to hear his voice, but worried, too. "This is a solo match. Isn't patching in kind of cheating?"

"Everyone else gets to talk to their teammates, why should you be on the outs because your mates got pinged?" Zane's weird sayings never sounded so good to my ears. "Hoi, Mate. Take the nature strip heading down to your west." I saw a green path and started walking down it. "It heads you down to Dusty Divot. You've got a right good angle now to snipe off any competitors downhill from you. Just watch out for the moving bushes. They're not your friends."

I jogged down the path, feeling more confident having my friends—my "mates"—at my back. I saw a moving bush and took a crack at it with a short-range weapon. A drone picked up the avatar and I had my third "kill" of the game. I checked my long-range sights and saw some moving targets down below. There were a few people building forts, and others chasing each other around. I felt a touch at my elbow and swung around, weapon drawn. I was face-to-face with an opponent dressed in plain army fatigues with a long-range weapon. She held her hands up as if in surrender. We couldn't communicate with each other with words, but motioned that we should team up and snipe the people down below together. "What do you guys think?" I asked my teammates through the headset.

"She's porkers. Don't listen to 'er," Zane warned.

"I think Zane means it's a trap. It's every player for himself or herself down there. She just doesn't have the weapon to take you out with yet," Jin explained. "Protect yourself."

I saw their point, but decided to trust her for now. She knew how to shoot long-range, and she had already picked off one of the shooters below. "I'm not really hitting anything. Any suggestions?"

"Get him in your sights," Jin said. I placed the target inside the crosshairs. "Now aim slightly higher to account for gravity." I moved it up just a touch. "Wait for it . . . NOW!" I let loose and it was a direct hit! The girl next to me gave me a high five. I was feeling great!

We continued to travel down toward the crater side by side, weapons drawn and firing at anything that moved around us. It was kind of beautiful the way nature had reclaimed the area and grown over all the waste and destruction when the meteor had hit. I saw a gold glow in the distance in the back of a truck bed and ran toward it, looking over at my new companion to see if she had seen it, too. She did and raced me to it. I picked up my pace once I saw she was trying to beat me to the chest, and when I came close enough, she stuck out her arm to hold me back. *So much for teaming up*, I thought. I pulled out my pickaxe and whacked her out of the way, leaping and somersaulting over another parked car to get there first. I opened the chest and discovered a couple of weapons and a shield, which I chugged in the safety of the truck bed.

The shield activated just in time, as my ally-turned-opponent jumped to the top of the truck bed with her weapons drawn. "Not today," I yelled, even though she couldn't hear me. I once again used my pickaxe and swept her off her feet, knocking her down, then used my new automatic weapon to wipe her out before her health could regenerate. Off she went in her drone. I gave her a little goodbye dance before jumping down off the truck and hitting up the buildings to find more loot. While I didn't find much, I kept track of the locations in my head as if I was filling in a blank map, knowing that next time, I'd have an advantage.

When I exited the building and tried to get my bearing, sniper shots rang out over my head. I ducked and fled the building, heading back up the slope. "I'm sniper-food down here," I called out. "Any suggestions?"

"Try Loot Lake," Jin suggested. "Go north-west 'til you hit water."

I made my way up the hill toward Loot Lake when another voice came through my headset, quiet but urgent. "Watch out. Ahead and to your left!" That was Jax's voice! I pulled out a short-range weapon and aimed as I scanned in front of me. I saw someone duck behind a tree and start shooting. I shot back, remembering to reload my weapons. "Throw up a wall," he suggested.

"Thanks, Jax," I replied, building a small protective fort. I had just put up the final wall when shots started coming in from all sides. "I think I'm done for here, guys. Any suggestions?"

"Build up," Jin said. "Just keep going up and over. When you get high enough, shoot down. It's always best to have higher ground."

I built until my resources were empty, then looked down to find my attackers had found someone else to pick on. I took a moment to refill my shield and apply some bandages for minor scrapes, then I tagged the wall of my first real fort just for fun. Then I jumped down to the ground and ran off toward Loot Lake. Suddenly, through my headset, I heard an argument break out.

"What in the world are you doing wearing those headsets?" Blaze demanded. "Are you helping her in a solo battle?"

"We're helping our mate, isn't that what we're supposed to do? Stick together?" Zane asked Blaze.

"This is cheating! I have a mind to tell Velasco what you're up to. You'll all get booted from the program. That's a third strike, you know!" Blaze was too angry to think clearly.

If we don't look good, she won't look good. And I wouldn't have done nearly this well in battle without them.

"We're working together," Jin said as he tried to appeal to her sense of reason. "Every other squad talks each other through the battle if they'd like. You'd prefer to leave Asha out here defenseless? That seems unfair, Blaze."

"Watch out behind you, Asha!" Zane called out. But it was too late. I had been so caught up in the argument, I lost focus. I was out.

As I climbed out of the avatar control station, Zane, Jin, and even Jax were there smiling at me. Zane gave me a huge hug. "You came in thirty-seventh! Good 'onya!"

"And you had five eliminations. That's awesome for your first solo!" Jin said, patting me on the shoulder.

"I couldn't have done it without you all," I said. I held out my hand to Jax and he shook it awkwardly. "Thanks for having my back."

"That's what we're here to do, right?" he replied, rubbing his neck and shrugging. "We should probably see where Blaze went. Maybe we can get to Velasco before she does and tell him our side of the story."

CHAPTER NINE: ZANE

Asha's success felt like a win for all of us. Velasco was nowhere to be found, so we headed back to our barracks. When I turned the corner, I froze. Blaze and the Sergeant were talking outside our rooms. "Steady on, mates," I said quietly. "We don't know what she's told 'im yet, but be prepared to talk about what a great team we are."

They both looked up as we approached. Velasco was smiling, which was a bit of a relief. "You've done a fine job, Asha."

"Thank you, sir," Asha replied modestly.

"That was excellent teamwork, all of you!" The sergeant beamed. "You've leveled up!" He turned to Blaze. "I think I'll include this in my report to your parents tonight. Nicely done!" He patted her on the back and she thanked him awkwardly. He had assumed it was all Blaze's idea, and she didn't even correct him, that double-crossing rat!

"I think we all did our part, sir," I interjected. I couldn't let him leave thinking Blaze had anything to do with Asha's success. "In fact, Blaze had just come in . . ."

Blaze interrupted me. "I'm sure the sergeant has better things to do than listen to us recount the glory of this battle, Zane." She flashed Sergeant Velasco her biggest smile. "Isn't that right, sir?"

"Always the thoughtful one, eh Blaze?" He smiled back, then addressed the rest of us. "Go celebrate with a nice dinner, and get a good night's sleep. You're gonna need it to start fresh in the morning. The playing field just got a little bit tougher, kids." He gave a quick wave and then he was off. Blaze shrugged and walked into our quarters, leaving the four of us staring after her in disbelief.

I was the first to speak. "Well, that was really something, wasn't it?"

"That girl is really something, taking credit for what you did, Asha," Jin said, shaking his head.

"She must really need her parents' approval badly if she would sacrifice her relationship with her teammates for it," Jax muttered. I nodded. He had a good point.

"Well, let's not let this ruin our celebration," Asha said cheerfully, instantly lightening the mood. "Who's up for sushi?"

We all agreed dinner sounded like a great idea and set off toward the cafeteria. Asha hesitated at the corner. "Do you think we should get Blaze?" she asked.

"I think she was right plain about who she wants by her side," I said, walking ahead. "She prefers to act alone, so she can eat alone."

The cafeteria was buzzing with activity while squads ate together and recounted their battles. It was amazing how no one mixed with others outside their squads, and none of us were tempted to break that trend. In just one day, we had already become a team. At least most of us had. I was the only one facing the door when Blaze walked into the cafeteria. She scanned the room and she finally found our table, her eyes catching mine. For a moment, it looked as though she wanted to join us. I hesitated a moment, then looked down, pretending I hadn't seen her.

Out of the corner of my eye, I saw Blaze gather her dinner and leave, probably taking her meal to her room. I didn't feel badly about it for a second.

CHAPTER TEN: BLAZE

I have to admit, my conversation with Sergeant Velasco was not my finest moment. But if I had it to do over again, I'd probably do the same thing. These raw recruits just didn't understand how important it was not only to act as a team, but to present ourselves as a team. They went behind my back to help Asha, which amounts to treason, really. But after the win, we had to present ourselves as a united front. It wasn't really lying. That's what those other kids didn't understand. I was willing to go down with the team as a team, so I accepted the praise with the team when it worked out okay. It would all even out in the end. That's what they didn't realize.

I ate my dinner alone in my room and left the dishes outside in the hallway for maintenance to collect on their nightly sweep. I went to bed early, and pretended to be asleep when Asha came into the room late. But afterward, I lay awake for hours, feeling angry, then guilty, then angry again in a vicious cycle until the morning announcement blared through the speakers.

I ran into Zane on the way to the restroom, but, like he had the night before in the cafeteria, he didn't even acknowledge me. I shrugged it off. If that was the way it was going to be, he should realize sooner rather than later that if it came down between him, a son of a rebel with no loyalty or training, and me, a third-generation soldier with ties to the top brass in this unit . . . well, it would be no contest.

I washed up quickly and headed to the avatar room before the rest of them were ready. I wanted a chance to regroup and figure out how to regain my position as leader. They may have leveled up the day before, but things were about to get tougher, and they were going to need me whether they knew it or not. As I waited for the doors to open, I thought about how I would handle it. In the end, I decided to apologize and ask for a second chance. When they filed into our control room behind me, I said my piece.

"About last night . . . I'm really sorry I didn't come clean with Velasco. It took me by surprise. All I could think about was how proud my parents would be when they heard we leveled up." They exchanged glances and the feelings of hostility I sensed from them seemed to soften. "If you want, I can go to him right now and tell him the truth . . ."

"Everyone, take your places, please! The Battle Royale is about to begin!" Velasco's voice boomed over the speakers. *Perfect timing*, I thought, patting myself on the back in my imagination.

"Let's get through this battle. We can talk about it when we're through," Zane said, climbing into his console. I smiled and did the same.

As my visor faded in, I noticed new instructions on the glass in front of me. There was a list of challenges to complete. A Battle Royale at this level wasn't necessarily more difficult to fight, but there were achievements we'd need to complete in order to rack up a good score. "Score two three-point baskets? I could do that in my sleep!" Jin cried out. "I like level two so far."

I looked at the rest of the list and quickly calculated the best way to achieve the most points in the shortest time. "I have a plan," I announced, then added: "If anyone wants to hear it."

"You're going to tell us anyway," Jax said in a monotone. I could tell he was rolling his eyes at me.

The battle bus winked into view. We sat in two rows facing each other. They were looking at me, ready to listen. I drew out a game plan that took each of the achievements into account, starting with a drop point and assigning jobs to each of us based on our skill set. Obviously scouting chests would go to Asha and shooting hoops would go to Jin, while sniping belonged to Jax. That left me and Zane to play wingman, making sure we had enough supplies and shields and had each other's backs. I was amazed they all agreed, and before we knew it, we were at the drop spot for Retail Row.

Although we had only been down to the island a few times before, it was starting to feel like a familiar routine. We went into free fall and our gliders deployed automatically. It was getting easier to drive my glider now, and we all touched next to the double-colored red and white house without a hitch. I entered through the front door while Zane went around to the garage and the rest of the team scouted the outside. Walking through the kitchen felt oddly familiar to me. It reminded me of the first house I could remember living in on an army base in Minnesota. The layout was almost exactly the same. I gathered supplies while I searched the bottom floor of the house, and paused to drink a shield in the bathroom. Zane and the rest kept up a constant chatter through our com, calling out weapons they had found.

Sounds of shots rang through my headset, followed by silence. "Everyone okay?" I whispered.

"Just a direct hit with my new super powerful weapon," Jax replied happily.

"Anyone else having as much fun as Jax?" I asked, trying to keep the mood light. They reported back with talk of the two chests they had opened and loot they had found, but there was something else. Something new that I couldn't put my finger on.

"I found an attic above the garage," Jin called out. "Asha, you're going to want to tag this. Can you get up here?"

I ran up to see it and arrived at the same time as Asha. Jin had broken the side wall of the attic, exposing it to the rest of Retail Row. Asha took out her paints and started spraying. In less than a minute, she had written: "The Impossibles Were Here!" With a satisfied final look at her work, she holstered her spray cans and jumped down to the ground. "My work is done here. What's next?"

Jin bounded down and headed toward the town center. "I saw a basketball court on the way down. Cover me. I'm going to shoot some hoops!" Zane and Asha ran at his sides and the three of them were goofing around together on their way to the court while Jax and I had their backs. They were laughing. That's what was different. We were all actually having fun!

Of course, that didn't last long. Shots rang out overhead, and Jax and I sprang into action. Jax pointed to a tower in the distance where another player was taking aim. He and I both fired, taking out the tower but not our opponent. We didn't get credit for a snipe, but we did neutralize the threat. We ran ahead to catch up and caught Jin sinking a basket and doing a backflip to celebrate.

Asha started a victory dance, but I put a stop to it. "Three chests and one basket down. Two chests, one basket, and one sniper elimination to go. We'll celebrate when we win." I knocked down the fence at the end of the basketball court for emphasis, and jumped down to the ground.

We spread out and moved through Retail Row, checking trucks, rooms, and hidden corners for chests, but they had all been opened. "If the chests are open, chances are there are people with weapons nearby, too," Zane reasoned. "Stay alert."

"There's a legendary!" Asha shouted. "Floor loot—right out in the open under the stairs!" I saw her run for it, then Zane knocked her out of the way. "*Oof!* What'd you do that for?"

Zane pointed to the roof of the stairwell where a spike trap had been placed. "It's a trap. Oldest trick in the book."

Relieved, we made our way more carefully through the rest of town, picking up spare materials. I walked into one of the stores and saw something glowing from behind a wall. "Hey, I think I found a chest!" I didn't wait for help. I hacked down the wall and there it was, gleaming and practically singing to me to open it. I placed the sniper in my pack and looted a small ammo box on my way out. This was like the most useful treasure hunt ever. I was having fun, too!

When I exited the building, I found my four squad-mates waiting for me outside. They were watching a fast-moving vehicle careening toward us. "What is that?" I asked.

Zane tilted his head sideways. "Looks an awful lot like a golf cart to me."

As it got closer, I could tell he was right. It was an All Terrain Kart. Two crazy drivers were doing donuts in the parking lot. "Those cadets are having way too much fun," I said, taking out my short-range weapon. "What do you say we take them out to teach them a lesson?" Zane agreed and we took aim as if they were moving targets at a carnival game.

"Easy peasy!" he called out after we hit them. "They never even saw us coming." They were just knocked down, not eliminated, but I didn't see any teammates rushing over to help them heal. We could have helped, but after all, this was a war game and they were technically the enemy. "What do you say we commandeer their vehicle, too?" Zane laughed.

Four of us piled into the ATK while Jax climbed on top. Zane was a crazy driver and took us on a wild ride. "Do you even know how to drive this thing?" I asked, holding on for dear life, forgetting for the moment that I was just controlling an avatar and wasn't really in the cart.

"Not bad for my first time driving, eh?" Zane said with a wink.

He took off toward Fatal Fields, but I stopped him. "It's too wide open over there. Let's head to the desert."

He shrugged and turned left. "Doesn't matter much to me, as long as I get to drive." He swerved to avoid a trap lying in the road. "You okay up there, Jax?" he asked.

"Never better," he replied happily. "Keep doing what you're doing."

We came to a road. "Anyone know where this leads?" Zane asked.

I looked around. "If I didn't know any better, I'd say Utah." Being an army kid had us road tripping more than anyone I'd ever met. I had been to all fifty states at least twice, but Utah's giant rock formations and land that looked like it went on forever made it my favorite.

Asha spoke up. "I don't know anything about Utah, but we're in Paradise Palms. This road should lead to a fancy club up ahead and . . ." she stopped mid-sentence and just pointed. I followed her finger and stared openmouthed at the giant statues up ahead. "Dinosaurs?"

Zane screeched to a stop and we all jumped out to get a better look, feeling more like tourists than warriors for a moment. My heavy backpack jolted my memory, though, and I pulled out my weapon in case we ran into trouble. Jax bounded up a long-necked dinosaur while the rest of us marveled at the giant statues from below.

"I have a line on someone. Anyone have a sniper I can use?" Jax called down. I threw down a bouncer and jumped up to hand the weapon to him, then slid down the neck of the dinosaur. "Yeehaaaa!" I cried out with glee. That call was one of my favorite things I learned from my cowgirl days in Wyoming.

We all seemed to hold our breath as Jax took aim and shot. A message flashed across my view screen. *Minka was sniped by Jax.* Jax let out a whoop and slid down the dinosaur's neck as well. We all high-fived each other. *I really have a great team*, I thought. That was the moment I felt sure this leadership role was really going to work out for me. We hopped back into the ATK, but hadn't gone far before Asha called to Zane to stop the cart. She jumped out and ran. Zane covered her, and actually knocked down a pair of cadets who were closing in on her. She got to a chest and opened it, and was about to grab the loot when two more cadets came out of the shadows toward her. "You got the last chest and completed the achievement. Leave the loot! Let's move!" Jin shouted. Asha sped back to the cart and we headed back down the road.

Safely inside the vehicle, Asha looked around. "Is this cheating? I mean, we're faster than everyone and it's a pretty big advantage . . ." I shrugged. There was nothing in the rule books against it. It seemed fine to me.

Suddenly, Asha slumped over in her seat. "She's been hit!" Jin cried out. He took out a kit and quickly healed her.

"Thanks," Asha sighed. "I needed that!" She looked around. "Where did that shot come from?"

In response, they heard a shot ring out through Jax's com. "She won't be doing that again this game!" A message appeared onscreen: *Jackie was sniped by Jax.* That made two snipes by Jax this game. He was rocking it!

Another message appeared onscreen: "Storm eye shrinks in three minutes."

"Step on it, Zane! We have to make it to the center of Paradise Palms before the eye shrinks," Asha said. "I just hope the basketball hoop there won't be crowded because that's where the eye is closing in."

We pulled up at a broken-down basketball court and Jin jumped out. "I've got this!" he called, but he leapt without looking. There were already two other cadets shooting hoops on the court. As long as they were shooting hoops, they weren't armed, I noticed. Asha and Zane noticed that as well. They took out the two distracted ballers and left them to be healed or left behind by their squad-mates while we gathered around Jin for his last shot. He missed the first two and took a deep breath before trying again. I noticed on the view screen we were five of only fifteen people left on the island. We had one snipe shot to go to make it a team total of three. Jin steadied his hand and kept missing. The storm eye was going to shrink again soon and we were running out of time.

"Asha, can you cover Jin while we take the last challenge?" I asked. She nodded and Jax, Zane, and I headed off to find some high ground we could shoot from. We were under the cover of some low bushes when I saw a team of four cadets up above us on a ledge. "We could take one of them out, but we need a plan," I said, thinking out loud.

Zane put his hand on Jax's shoulder. With his other hand, he pointed to Jax's weapon, then to the team on the ledge. "I'll distract them. You go for the kill," he said.

"You'll be eliminated," Jax said plainly.

Zane shrugged. "But we'll win the challenge," he replied. I could have stopped him, but I didn't have any better ideas, and I certainly wasn't about to put myself in the line of fire.

Zane counted to three and ran into the clearing. The four cadets took the bait and fired on Zane, knocking him down and then eliminating him completely. Jax didn't wait a moment. He stood up from behind the rock, set his sights, and fired, taking down a cadet named Malik who tumbled off the cliff and was eliminated. The others fired on Jax, who took a hit and fell next to me behind the rock. At the same time, a shout came through my com. Jin had scored the basket. We had completed the challenge! I ran to meet them at the court, where we three celebrated before being ambushed by two other players heading to shoot their last baskets before the storm eye closed for good. We didn't win, but we were victorious!

CHAPTER ELEVEN: JAX

I climbed out of my pod and stretched my aching muscles. My body was spent, and my brain was feeling pretty fried, too. At least the headaches had stopped. We were getting used to having our brains jacked, and it felt like we were getting used to each other, too. Most of us, anyway. I mean, what was up with Blaze taking off without healing me? That was cold. Especially after she took credit for helping Asha. And she didn't own up to distracting her so she got eliminated the night before. Just plain selfish, if you ask me, which no one really did, come to think of it. In the end, I stayed in longer than she did, which kind of felt like a win.

Everyone filed out of their pods and into the center of the avatar room, awaiting the results. We clustered together with some of the folks I had recognized by their avatars in the game. I didn't know any of them by name, though. It was weird knowing we had more contact with our fellow cadets as avatars than in real life.

A roar went up as the stats came up on the video display. I-28 came in fourth. Not a bad showing, I thought. Velasco explained we were given points for completing the challenge and additional points for how many people were left when we were eliminated. The top three teams leveled up, which made us the top seed for the next round.

"Moving forward," Velasco boomed above the noise of the crowd, "you'll spend the next two weeks training at your level with your squad. For everyone but the top three, that means playground, skirmishes, and strategy classes. Teams one, two, and three, please stay behind and we will discuss paring down your group to four squad members." He waited for the crowd's surprise and conversation to die down, then added: "You are all dismissed for the rest of the day. Dinner is at eighteen-hundred hours in the mess hall."

The crowd thinned as the rest of the squads left. I noticed Blaze and Asha were off in a corner, arguing. "You just left him there?" Asha shouted.

"I thought he had been eliminated, I guess," Blaze replied. "I mean, you shouted, so I ran over. What if you needed help?"

If I hadn't guessed they were talking about me, Blaze's guilty glance in my direction would have clinched it.

"Being part of a team means looking out for each other." Asha wouldn't let it go.

"It's fine. We'll do better next time," I said quietly. Even though it wasn't really fine what Blaze did, and it would take a long time for me to get past it. I just wanted Asha to drop it and go back to being her annoyingly happy self again. It was weird to see her angry when she was usually so perky and positive. It made me feel uncomfortable.

Blaze took a deep breath and turned to me. "I'm sorry I left you there, okay?"

She didn't seem sorry at all, to be honest. "Whatever. Let's just drop it," I shrugged. As I walked away, I looked up and saw Velasco staring at us. The room was pretty empty at that point. He had probably heard the whole conversation, but there was nothing I could do about it. If he did, the next step was his.

I saw Zane and Jin up ahead. They were leaving the avatar room. I wanted to catch up to them but wasn't sure what to say. I kind of hovered nearby and waited for an opening. Jin was recapping how he hit the final shot just when he was about to lose hope. He was talking with his hands in an animated way. I could tell he was excited. He caught my eye and then just stopped and nudged Zane. "Um," I began. I rubbed the back of my neck. It was a habit I had when I wasn't sure what to say, which was most of the time. "Hey."

They both smiled and waited for me to catch up with them. "Thanks for what you did back there," I said to Zane.

"No worries, mate. I took one for the team. You'd 'a done the same for me, right-o?" Zane slapped me on the back in what I took to be a friendly way.

"Yeah, guess so," I replied dumbly. Then I turned to Jin. "Great job with the hoops." Jin smiled broadly. He seemed pretty proud of his achievement, which was nice to see.

"That was pretty radical how you rode on top of the vehicle like that," Jin said.

"And your sniping skills are spot-on," Zane added.

I felt pretty good, too, I realized. I didn't have anything more to say, so I was content just to walk along beside them as they went back to their conversation, recounting every second of the battle.

We arrived at our quarters and saw a group standing outside their room, just next door to us. "Hey there, Kevin," Zane said cheerfully.

The kid who was clearly Kevin shrank back nervously. "Um, hey there. Guess we're neighbors, huh? Sorry about before on the train . . ." I could tell he was about to chatter on nervously if someone wasn't going to stop him. He was the opposite of me. I always clam up when I don't know what to say. Kevin was the kind of person who would spit out a constant stream of words hoping that any of them might be the right thing to say.

"No worries, mate. I was just messing with you, really. First day jitters and all," Zane said. When he arrived here on the base, he seemed so quietly suspicious, as if he didn't know what to expect. Now he seemed to be enjoying himself.

"So you were the fourth-place team?" Kevin's teammate asked. "I'm Malik, by the way."

That name sounded familiar, then I remembered the flash on the screen after my last snipe. "I'm Jax. Sorry about that last kill."

Malik shook my hand, grinning. "I'm sorry I took down your friend. That was a pretty lively battle. Smart move sacrificing one of your own as a distraction."

"That was all Zane's idea," I admitted, hoping the rest of the squad would take over the conversation.

"Hey, so what happens with your squad now that you're moving up and becoming a team of four?" Jin asked.

Malik and Kevin both smiled. "It worked out great, actually," Kevin said. "We had someone who wasn't a great fit and . . ."

Malik cut him off. "They don't need to know all our secrets, Kevin. But it did work out well in the end." Malik opened the door to their quarters and was about to go in, but turned back. "In case you didn't know, HQ sees and hears everything that goes on both on the battlefield and in our quarters. Just because you close a door or speak softly, don't assume Velasco and the rest of them aren't listening." They waved goodbye and headed into their rooms, leaving the three of us wondering what else we didn't know about this place and which one of us would get cut when the time came to level up.

CHAPTER TWELVE: JIN

I knew it. I knew they were watching us everywhere. Why wouldn't they? We were in their world and we had signed away all our rights to privacy when we joined up. It would have been silly to think they just meant they would watch us while we were on the battlefield and in training. But one thing wasn't clear: Why? What kind of information were they collecting on us? Was it just to see how we were doing in our training, or were they looking for something more? In some places, I could see it made sense to keep an eye on us. Like Zane, for instance—a rebel on the inside could be seen as a threat to their whole organization. But what about kids like me? I'd rather not let any of the top brass know I had my suspicions about this place. I'd have to keep my ideas to myself for now.

We ate dinner at the mess hall as a squad. We each grabbed plates of food from different countries and placed them in the center of the table so we could try as many of them as possible. I was a big fan of the Brazilian cheese bread, and thought the Texas chili was pretty tasty. But I couldn't bring myself to taste Canadian Poutine, which looked like French fries topped with cheese and sauce, even though Jax liked it so much he went back for seconds. Without really talking about it, we kept the conversation light, talking only about the food and comparing it to the food back home. It was the first time we had all just had a normal conversation, and it felt good just to chat and eat like I was back at school.

When it was time for dessert, Jax and Blaze insisted my life wouldn't be complete without tasting a banana split. But before I could go back to the buffet, Officer Gremble appeared at our table looking serious. He greeted Blaze first. "Sergeant Velasco asked me to send for you and your squad. He has some important news to share."

We all exchanged worried looks. We were all in a pretty good mood after our solid ranking in the afternoon battle, but what if that hadn't been enough to get us out of the doghouse? We got up and followed Gremble out of the mess hall. "We'll need to have a spokesperson. I'll do the talking," Blaze whispered when the officer was out of earshot.

Jax rolled his eyes, which showed me just how much respect he had for her. I looked at Asha and shrugged. She smiled back. "Maybe it's good news." I liked her optimism, but I still expected the worst.

We followed the officer up a flight of stairs to a new area of the compound we hadn't seen before. He approached a locked door which opened with a click after it scanned his eye. The door opened into a regular office building with actual windows that looked out onto the desert landscape. The bright natural sunlight was refreshing, but our view didn't last long. He ushered us into a very plush windowless office with leather couches, house plants, and a large mirror across one long wall. The officer asked us to take a seat, then he left to get the Sergeant. It looked like the principal's office at school. That made me feel even more like we were in trouble. After what Kevin and Malik had said earlier, we didn't dare speak, knowing they were probably listening or even watching us as we waited.

I almost didn't recognize Sergeant Velasco when he walked in. He was wearing a short-sleeved shirt and jeans. "I'm sorry about my outfit," he explained as he sat down in the leather chair opposite me. "Under normal circumstances, I head home after the battles are over, but . . . well . . . let me back up." Now I was really worried. He had come back in just to talk with us. We must really be in trouble.

He waved his hand and a screen went down on the blank wall opposite the mirrored wall with a frozen snapshot from the battle. "Anyone recognize this shot?" he asked.

"That's where Jax sniped someone. Minka, I recall," Zane answered. Blaze gave him a dirty look. She had wanted to be the only one who spoke, but Zane kept his eyes on Velasco, ignoring her glare.

"Very good, Zane. Yes, Minka was knocked down by Jax, but she was the last of her team to go down. Due to a glitch in the system, the drone never arrived to collect her avatar," he explained as the still image sprang to life. The scene replayed, showing a surprised Minka stand up, collect her weapon, and run off toward the basketball court where Jin was shooting hoops. Minka went on to complete the challenge for her team, earning them third place in the competition.

"They didn't earn that win!" Zane exclaimed.

"Precisely. You get to level up," Velasco explained.

We all looked at each other, grinning. We had just gone from having the most impossible odds to being in the top three of level two. Everyone wore an expression of surprise mixed with relief and pride. But then he continued in a more serious tone. "As you may recall, however, that means you get to elect a leader and you have to pare down to a squad of four." He waited for the news to sink in.

My heart sank into my feet as I looked around at the group. Someone would be leaving while another would be the new leader. I didn't have the heart to choose. Would anyone else? "Ultimately, it will be our choice, but we like to take your votes into account."

"If it's your choice, why let us vote at all?" Jax said sullenly, crossing his arms in front of his chest. Sometimes he acted more like a rebel than Zane did.

"Well, Jaxon, believe it or not, we respect you. You see things that we don't. You experience things together that we can't measure. We take that into account very seriously," the sergeant said. "But we also see things that you don't, and those need to be counted as well. We consider ourselves very fair here." Jax just rolled his eyes. The sergeant got up and handed us each a tablet. On the screen were two words: LEAD and LEAVE, with a place for us to type in a name next to each. He walked to the door. "I'll be back in five minutes. Feel free to talk among yourselves. There are no microphones or hidden cameras in here."

The door closed with a click, leaving the five of us sitting in silence, holding our tablets. "Okay, what just happened here?" Asha asked. "So we won, but now we have to choose? How do we decide?"

I looked around the room, convinced Velasco was lying and he was in another room watching our every move, but I didn't see a camera. "Before we start to talk about it, do you really think they're not watching us?" I asked.

"He said there were no cameras or microphones. He didn't say they weren't watching us." Zane pointed to the mirror on the far wall. "One-way observation mirror," he explained.

I wasn't surprised, but wasn't going to respond. So that was how it was going to be. Constant observation. I decided to keep my mouth shut and turn to the tablet. It didn't take me long to make my choice. I saw the others turn to their tablets and finish just as quickly. Clearly, they had the same thoughts.

As soon as we all put our tablets down, Velasco walked back into the room. "Thank you for voting, and thank you for coming in. Your vote matched our own." He walked over to Blaze and shook her hand. She took his hand smiling broadly, confident he was congratulating her. "I'm so sorry, Blaze. But it was unanimous."

Her smile faded into a look of shock. "Wait, what? I'm . . . out?" She looked around at all of us. "And it was unanimous?"

Velasco gently took Blaze's elbow and helped her to her feet. "I'm sorry, Blaze, really I am. I know how much this program means to you and your family. But it's just the fit . . ."

Blaze wrenched her arm away from him. "The fit?" She screamed. "I'll say it was a bad fit. I've been in military training my whole life, while this sad group of misfits just showed up with no clue. You know how impossible it is to work with people like that?" She picked up my tablet and looked at it, then at me. "Seriously, Jin? I had your back. I told you guys exactly what to do. We failed because you didn't do any of it." She threw the tablet onto the ground where it shattered. Then she scrunched up her eyes and balled her fists and jumped up and down on the broken pieces of the tablet, screaming while we all just stared at her.

When she was done, Jax spoke up quietly, as always. "We didn't fail. We succeeded because we worked together. You failed because you let us down. A real leader wouldn't walk away after their teammate got shot down. A real leader would get all the facts before making a plan. And a real leader would apologize when they knew they made a mistake."

It was the most any of us had heard Jax speak at one time, but his words hit home for all of us. Blaze, however, couldn't bring herself to accept his words as the truth. She threw her hands up in the air. "Whatever. If that's what you think of me, there is no way we could ever work together as a team." She walked toward the door. "I'm out of here. I'm going back to pack my things. You can send my new assignments to my old quarters. I'll be happy to be rid of you people and start fresh with a new squad." She tried to tug open the door, but it wouldn't budge. The sergeant pressed a button on his wristwatch and the door opened slowly. Blaze slipped through before the door was fully open, leaving the rest of us in stunned silence.

The sergeant cleared this throat and we all looked up at him. "So, about your new squad leader," he said, turning to Zane. "The job is yours if you'll accept it."

CHAPTER THIRTEEN: ZANE

When Velasco offered me the position as squad leader, I just nodded dumbly. I couldn't turn it down, but I couldn't understand why I had been chosen—and all of them, my mates and the sergeant, had voted for me. Well, everyone but Blaze, who had clearly voted for herself. I accepted congratulations from Jin, Asha, and Jax in a daze, then they were dismissed back to our quarters while I was asked to stay back for a moment. The sergeant and I sat back down in the soft leather chairs, face-to-face.

"So, what do you think?" Velasco asked me.

"I'm honored my mates have chosen me. Fair dinkum! But strewth—I'm not sure I'm worthy. If I hadn't seen them vote, I'd have thought you promoted me so you could keep a better eye on me. I get a fair suspicion you and the blokes behind that one-way mirror don't right trust me." I figured I'd be straight up with him from the start.

The sergeant sat back and stretched his arms and placed them behind his head. His body language was a classic pose of strength and having nothing to hide, but he looked too uncomfortable. He quickly put his hands down by his side, realizing I wasn't buying his act. "Your mates, as you call them, all chose you. Except Blaze, of course. And we saw you take the lead quite a few times down there on the island and here at HQ. We think you have true leadership potential, Zane."

"Thank you, but you didn't answer the second half of my question." I knew I wouldn't get the chance to ask again, so I pressed him for an answer. "D'ya trust me?"

He leaned forward in his chair with his elbows on his knees. That meant he was trying to seem honest and open. "No, Zane. We don't. But we don't have a good reason to trust you, do we? Your parents spend a great deal of time causing trouble for us, and even opposed this program. They've cost us a lot of money over the years with their protests and blockades. My superiors didn't want to let you into the program at all, but I liked your application. Not sure I believed all of it, but I liked it."

I replied honestly. "It took a lot to put those words down on paper. If that ever fell into my parents' hands, they'd have my hide."

"You told us in your essay that you wanted to learn about what they were fighting against firsthand to decide for yourself what side you wanted to take in this fight. That application was signed by your parents. Do you mean to tell me they signed your application but never read your essay?"

I felt certain if I looked him in the eye, he would guess the truth, so I kept looking down. "I don't think I should talk with you about my application anymore, sir."

Velasco moved in closer, forcing me to look up. "We can put this conversation on the shelf for now, but can you at least reassure me that your interest in this program is real? Is any of what you wrote true?"

"Yes. It's all true, but no, my parents aren't clear on why I'm here, and I'd rather keep it from them," I said honestly.

Satisfied, Velasco stood up. I followed him to the door. "That's all I need to hear," he said. "For now. But I'm keeping my eye on you. In my eyes, once a rebel, always a rebel."

I left to head back to our quarters, hoping Blaze had already cleared out. It would take some time before any of us wanted to face her again. But I hadn't gone more than a few steps down the hallway when I was joined by Jax, Asha, and Jin. "I thought you'd be back at the rooms by now."

Jax rubbed his neck uncomfortably. Asha pointed to a window set into the wall behind me. It was the back end of the one-way mirror with a view of the room we had just been sitting in. "You were right about the mirror," she said. "We stayed to see if we could hear the conversation, which we could. I'm sorry we listened in."

I took a deep breath and nodded.

"Your parents don't even know you're here, do they?" Jin asked softly.

I was about to protest, but thought better of it. Better they knew the truth. They were my mates now and I didn't want any secrets between us. I shook my head no. I was about to tell them the whole story, then looked around. "I know the walls have ears around here, but do you think there's somewhere we can go that's a little more private?"

"I know just the place," Asha said. "Follow me."

We followed her back down to the general quarters. There was no eye scan needed to exit the area. We went through a maze of hallways. I heard Asha counting under her breath as we passed each door. "Thirty-one. Thirty-two. Thirty-three! It's this one!" she said proudly and tugged on the door to open it. We walked into a gigantic gym. The air hummed with vibrations from a series of motors located somewhere beyond the walls of the room. Teams were running through the course in real life, not using their avatars, going around obstacles, sliding under impossibly low barriers, and tagging gold chests. "This is the training gym," she explained, speaking above the noise. "I took my test to get in as an alternate here. It's so loud, there's no way we could be recorded."

We moved over to a bunker area. Jin vaulted himself up on top of it and we all followed him by climbing up a rock wall on the other side. It gave us a view of the practice field, and anyone watching would assume we were either spying on the competition or creating a strategy.

"So, you were going to tell us your life story," Jax urged me to begin.

"Right. To answer your question, Jin, no, my parents don't know I'm here."

Asha looked worried "Where do they think you are?"

"When I saw the call for recruits and I reached the right age, I created a fake application to a fake school that I knew my parents would approve of. They signed it, then I changed the application and the essay and sent it out to HQ."

"How is that possible?" Asha asked.

I shrugged. "Ever since they joined the revolution, they've been taking off, leaving me home with the housekeeper. They'd leave money for groceries and signed me up for school. I rarely saw them. It wasn't much of a life, really. I used to believe in the revolution because they did, but as I got older, I started to question what they were fighting for." I had never told anyone my story before. It was hard, but it also felt good to open up about it.

"Wow," Jin shook his head, laughing. "You really are a rebel! You're rebelling against the rebellion."

I joined in, realizing it felt good to laugh, and it felt great to have someone to laugh with for a change. I looked at my new mates: Jin, who believed there was something more to this place than the leaders were letting on. Asha, who wanted to break free and see the world—and maybe make it a little brighter with some well-placed spray paint. And Jax, who, despite his looks and his reputation, seemed like a good guy. We all had our own battles to fight that we were bringing to this Battle Royale. These were the people on my squad. They had proven that they would always have my back just as I swore to have theirs. We were a good, solid team. We were mates, on and off the battlefield. And I couldn't wait for the next Battle Royale to begin!